THE
POMPITOUS
OF LOVE

Thank you so much.

Joe Rukeyser

Stories
Joseph Rukeyser

The Pompitous of Love
Copyright © 2022 Joseph Rukeyser

ISBN: 978-1-954517-29-5

Cover design by Stephanie Weinberger

Designed and produced by:
Indie Author Books
12 High Street, Thomaston, Maine
www.indieauthorbooks.com

Printed in the United States of America

For Roberta

Contents

THE POMPITOUS OF LOVE

Contents

THE MATING HABITS OF WHOOPING CRANES

Unlike whooping cranes, which, according to his daughter Pru, mate for life, Fat Dan Feldman is hopelessly, shamelessly, serially nonmonogamous, and radically unfaithful.

Pru is a precocious third grader who now lives with her mother, Dan's first wife, in Parsippany, New Jersey. Dan sees Pru on alternate weekends and on the high holy days when they fall in odd-numbered months.

Dan is fast approaching fifty and would be the first to admit that he is the sole cause of the impending demise of his second marriage. He is just wired differently. He has a reflexive, sub-cognitive nerve circuit that instantaneously transmits nubile female images from his eyes directly to his loins and then up to his heart, entirely bypassing and willfully subverting the scrutiny of any higher rational brain centers.

He's no dummy. He majored in journalism at Hopkins. He teaches creative writing at Forest Hills High School to rather well-off adolescents whose parents both read hardcover books and pay cash for their children's orthodontia. He likes it all well enough on most days, and on the others, he quite adequately pretends to do so.

His adorable two-year-old twins, Max and Minnie, share a room in their three-bedroom apartment in Hollis, Queens.

When Dan met his current wife, Mirabelle, a chaste, thin-lipped woman of thirty-four, he thought she was like a rare and outstanding kosher cabernet: a woman with a big nose and a full body.

Mirabelle now sleeps each night in her own bedroom, claiming that his snoring drives her insane. Dan is sure, though, that this condition befell her long before he met her on J-Date.com shortly over three years ago.

What *does* drive Dan insane now, assuredly, is the smooth curve of his "Fit Before Fifty" aerobics yoga instructor's bottom. She is tight, trim, and twenty-two. Though, admittedly, he knows she is so totally not interested in him and totally not even remotely within his reach.

Soma Fitzgerald McCoy, though, the new true love of his life, is palpably within his reach. On her Facebook page, she bears a remarkably striking resemblance to a twentyish Valerie Bertinelli. Her raven hair, her lips like glazed raspberries, and her eyes like wet walnuts have captured his yearning heart.

She is, justifiably, an unbelievably remarkable woman. A former Fulbright Scholar with a degree in helping others, she volunteers at the local hospice three evenings a week and serves meals in a mobile soup kitchen on the other two nights. She loves dancing in the rain and says her favorite food is "to be surprised by anything you would like to cook for me."

Soma has sent Dan a warm and enthusiastic "I'm All Yours" response to his personal profile posting on MysteryMeet.com: The dot-com you need "when your life deserves more than just a match!" Which is exactly what Dan desires and feels he deserves: to experience once again that florid flush of gland-grinding, full-throated, old-time, real-time lust.

In a flurry of fervent texts over the last few days, Soma has promised him all of that and more.

She has it all and is willing to share: the allure of girlish innocence, the tenderness of vulnerability, and the full promise of luscious, unbridled abandon.

They have agreed to meet this coming Wednesday night at Sweet Basil in the West Village after her regularly scheduled monthly blood donation at Children's Hospital.

This meet-up, of course, has little chance of actually happening. Soma, you see, has sent Dan a text this afternoon, describing in detail what she will be wearing when they meet, and the notification has popped up on his iPhone. This has gladdened his heart.

At the very same instant, though, in the rolling hills of Parsippany, the same text notification has appeared on his laptop. The very same laptop he loaned to Pru this weekend so that she could work on her research project on the mating habits of whopping cranes for her third-grade class.

Pru asks her mom what a "cream-colored, crocheted cami you could just die for" might be.

And her mom, with great gratification, immediately places a call to Mirabelle, who packs Dan's underwear, a toothbrush, one clean button-down shirt, his rumpled collection of *Sports Illustrated Swimsuit* issues, and his bundle of anime cartoon comic books into an overnight bag.

She places these items along with a creased coupon for a one-time-only, two-for-one discount on White Castle hamburgers; a business card with the phone number of Myron Rosenblatt, her attorney; and a new edition of *A Dummy's Guide to Matrimony, Volume 2: From Acrimony to Alimony,* then leaves the overnight bag in the building lobby with Enrique, their implacable and well-muscled doorman, who, no doubt, has long seen all of this coming.

A Sudden Change in the
Weather at Weeping Rock

Harris and Cortina sat at a table near the door of the National Park Service Visitor Center, a short walk from the Weeping Rock trailhead. A plate of pancakes with butter and syrup was in front of each of them.

Their clothing was soaked through. Boots filled with mud. They looked bedraggled. Shaken.

Men and women in expensive-looking hiking gear and sleek backpacks came in through the open door, sunglasses set back atop their heads. They looked around the room and smiled at the couple and the uneaten plates of pancakes, as if the two were unfamiliar guests at a wedding party.

Harris poured syrup over the cakes. It trickled down over the edges.

Cortina did not look up from her plate. Her hair dripped in her lap.

"You should eat something," he said to her.

She shook her head. "I can't," she said.

Harris poured himself a second cup of coffee and lifted the pot toward her. She shook her head again.

When he put the pot down, she picked it up and poured a cup for herself.

"We should talk," he said.

"No," she told him.

He looked at her. She didn't look up. He knew it was over between them.

They'd made love the night before, in Bullhead City, in the back bedroom of her mother's double-wide, and then they'd slept late. They had to hurry to get on the road up to Zion.

Neither of them liked to feel pressured or rushed.

Cortina's mother worked at a casino in Laughlin, on the Nevada side of the Colorado River.

Just the day before, she had taken them to the casino for breakfast in the employees' cafeteria. Later, they swam in the river. The floodgates at Lake Mead had opened and they were carried easily downriver a few miles in the swift, brown current.

Downstream, Harris caught the edge of a wooden post of a partly submerged dock and reached his arm out to Cortina. She grabbed hold of his hand, and he held her tight. He laughed out loud like a child. They both did.

And then they walked up along the road and jumped back in the river again.

It was almost noon when they reached the parking area at the Weeping Rock trailhead. It would be three hours up to the East Rim, into Hidden Canyon, and another three back down.

Cortina had taken the same hike once before. The path was narrow—two yards wide at its widest.

Switchbacks crisscrossed the steep face of the mountain.

Cortina led. Single file. She called back to Harris, telling him the names of every tree and rock formation they passed on the way up: Kaibab limestone. Fremont cottonwoods. Quaking aspen. Utah juniper. Bristlecone pine. Navajo sandstone.

He followed in her footsteps as best he could.

In the canyon above the rim, protected from the wind, they drank the last of the water she had packed.

Harris, his legs covered in a fine red dust, imagined himself as a free young man who might once have lived and walked like the wind among these sacred sandstone canyons, across the plateaus, and down along the creeks in the valleys. This place begged to be worshipped.

When the sun traversed the rim, Cortina said they needed to head back down. They walked on the same trail they'd come up. Harris had hoped there would be another easier trail down.

They'd been together for about a year. They talked books. Shared pizzas and salads. They once took a weekend trip to Block Island, rode rented bikes, and bought rolls at a roadside bakery.

They were both reading *Blindness* then. She had recommended it to him. She liked Saramago's writing, though Harris found his style unnecessarily cumbersome.

Cortina had two children in their teens. They lived with her. They spoke badly about their father's new wife, with whom they spent weekends before she became pregnant, after which they felt they were no longer welcome.

He found the children hard to be around. Cortina knew that. She said he would get used to them over time. That they meant well, though Harris doubted that was true.

Down from the rim, they walked in shade. There was the rock face on one side and nothingness on the other. Far below, cars were leaving the park.

Harris's boots slipped occasionally on the downward slope. Cortina told him to keep a safer distance behind her.

There'd been a magnetic rush between them when they'd first met. An outsized hunger for each other.

She had a literary mind. Made references to authors and books he'd not read. She hated Hemingway. He suspected it was the man's matter-of-fact unfaithfulness rather than his writing that she disliked. She abhorred Roth. He sensed a peremptory rebuke in that, which he took personally.

Farther down the trail, the wind picked up. An updraft. The trail was shadowed by tall, darkening clouds.

Cortina unstrapped her backpack and removed a poncho, which she put on. She had not packed one for him. It snapped in the wind. He had not thought to bring one for himself.

A single crack of thunder. Rain began to fall.

Pebbles skittered down the mountain face from above. They walked down a few yards, no more than ten or fifteen, looking for some shelter. There was none.

Larger stones began to fall in the sheeting rain. Moments later, rocks the size of coconuts tumbled down past them. Water sluiced around their feet. Harris felt a tightness in his chest.

She screamed at him. "Turn around, go back up!"

Boulders the size of steamer trunks clattered and bounced around them. He shuddered in horror as each one passed.

"I can't do it," he told her.

"Just listen to me, damn it, we have to find some cover."

"Where?"

"Up there," she said, pointing to an outcropping of rock they had passed. He did as she said.

"Get down in there! Make room for me and don't move!"

Whole sections of the rock face split off. They slid down the mountainside, tumbling out and hitting the side again lower down, cracking in pieces, some landing on the switchbacks and others bringing down trees and shattering at the foot of the mountain.

Harris's breath came in short, panicked gulps. He forced himself back against the rock, stunned by the nearness of death, the reality and imminence of it. At any moment, they could be crushed or swept out into the nothingness.

He waited only for the next moment to come, then for that moment to pass.

When the rain finally stopped, the sky cleared and brightened. Waterfalls broke out through crevices in the rock face.

"Now," she said. "Let's go down now."

She walked down ahead of him. He sensed she was crying.

He flew home to New York alone. She drove the rental car back to Kingman.

He saw her once again. A chance meeting on one of the avenues in New York, uptown near the Met. She had let her hair grow out to a soft and appealing shade of gray.

It was cold, and they spoke for only a few minutes before she turned and took the arm of the tall, slender man she had been walking with.

On the Third Day

On the Third Day, God created the seas. And the seas covered the entire earth. And it was good. Not exactly one hundred percent good, but *okay* good.

It was all according to the design specs. But now, seeing it in real life, after having created the dark and the light, and the firmament and the earth, the seas were just...water. And so, His shoulders drooped, and a frown came over His thin, innocent, boyish face.

The water looked great. Don't get him wrong. It was clear and blue, and He could see his reflection on it and his toes all the way down to the bottom of the deepest, deepest part. This was, of course, before He created microplastics, and oil spills, and sulfates, and pop-tops, and algal blooms.

But the design flaw He saw in the immense flat expanse way out to the edge was that the water on one side of the earth was getting way too hot while the other side got so cold that you couldn't even dip your big toe in it. So He gave the earth a little nudge and it started to spin, and lo and behold, the spin made the winds, and they made the water mix around, and that made the currents, like the one he called the Antarctic Circumpolar Current. And He saw that the currents were good.

And while he was figuring out what to create next, He skimmed a few rocks into the water, watching how they bounced and plunked in, and made the water kind of ripple out in circles. And He saw that the ripples were good.

In fact, they were so totally cool that he was glad He had created them, and so He dumped in like a ton of really big rocks and eureka—He had made waves, and He said to Himself "Eureka."

This was actually the first time He had come up with that word, and He would no doubt use it again when creating Mallomars, and origami, and strawberry rhubarb pie, and polynomials, and those little helicopter thingies from the trees you can stick on your nose.

Eureka! he thought. The waves crashed up against the rocks, and he kept chucking in more and more rocks until voilà, the waves got really huge and started making groovy sounds He had never heard before. He made up new words like *dude* and *epic* and *gnarly* and *totally tubular* and *bikinis,* even.

So while He was grooving to the sound of the waves, He realized He was getting no work done, and He knew His father would get on his case about that. It hit him that He had, like, only four more days for the whole project, three if you subtracted Sunday, and His father would call him a slacker, like after He had let Mars—or was it Mercury?—nearly burn to a crisp like a cinnamon raisin bagel left in the toaster oven too long while you were in the other room watching TV.

So the waves kept crashing and smashing and pulverizing the big rocks until the pieces got so teeny-tiny they started making sand and islands that stuck up out of the water like dunes. When you walked on them, the sand would get in your sandals and get stuck between your toes, and then you would track it into the kitchen and your mother would completely lose it on you about the mess you were making on the floor she had just cleaned and she'd say, "You had better clean that up, mister, before your father gets home."

And so, God was a little unhappy. He was under a great deal of pressure. The workload was huge. There were scads of protogalaxies on His to-do list waiting for him back at the office.

But then a tiny voice whispered in His ear, "Listen, God—chill. No biggie, man. This sandy beach thing is awesome. So, like, kick back, man, you earned it. Sure, you've got stuff to do, but there's more to life than just work."

And so, God paused. He cleared a place in the sand and sat and watched the huge curling, white-foam-topped turquoise waves pound against the shore, and He smelled the salty air. He saw the weightless mist rise and make clouds and saw how the breezes would blow them around, and He thought about how people, when He got around to creating people, could bring their lunches and bags of potato chips and beer in Budweiser coolers and spend an afternoon in the summer and pay someone $25 or some outrageous amount just to park their car in a gravelly lot, and they would have to walk up the wooden path just to get to the water and get splinters in their feet, and then the seagulls would come when they weren't looking and break open the bags of Cheetos and get the sand all over them so they couldn't chew them anymore without grinding their teeth and spitting them out, and then the mosquitoes and greenheads would come and the people would have to pack everything up before it rained, then go home and watch TV or mow the lawn or walk the dog or do homework or the laundry before they took a nap on the couch before dinner.

And God saw that it was good. And He was happy, and in a micro-fraction of a milli- milli-God-second, he turned to digging holes and planting gobs of quinoa, acorns, marigolds, zucchini, and coconuts all over the place.

And there was evening, and there was morning, the Third Day. And it was good.

A Day at Hershey Park

Jack Benson, if he was asked, would say he felt pretty good about himself. He had never been much bothered about money. He did okay. He'd never wanted to be rich. He figured he'd get a job, have a family, make a living, and set aside a little for the future. He never thought much about making a lot of money or success or even what that might mean.

Now, looking back, he knows he could have paid more attention to things like that. But he didn't, and that was that.

He takes off his shoes by the door, hangs his heavy coat on the hook on the wall, and drops his key on the counter. He relights the stove under the cold coffeepot.

Late-afternoon light slants through the kitchen window. He sighs and sits down at the table. The worn wicker seat stretches and creaks. His hands are still cold from the walk. The sun is pleasant, though too weak to coax the stiffness out of his old bones.

He'd walked to the bank when it opened this morning. They'd be closing the branch near him on Main Street at the end of the month. The ATM too, but he'd never used it.

Next month, he'll have to walk a mile more to the other branch out by the top of King Street. At least, he figures, the walk back home from the new branch will be downhill and he could stop by the Dunkin' Donuts, where he could sit for a few minutes, get warm, maybe buy a coffee, and watch the townies in their caps with the names of naval vessels and service insignia and such embroidered on them, retelling stories around the table in the corner, and pass by them on his way to the for-customer-use-only bathroom.

On the line at the bank's coin machine, two women were ahead of him, talking about the bank closing. "It's all money and politics," the tall one said. "Nobody cares about people anymore."

"Oh please, Marie. Get a grip," said the other one, "It's just a damn bank. You're always thinking everyone's out there waiting to get you."

"All's I know," said tall Marie, "is someone's making money off this, and no one's sending *me* a check in the mail."

The women finished. Collected their tally slips. Jack emptied his ziplock bag of coins into the machine. By habit, he checked the coin reject slot like he used to do with the old pay phones on the street, when they still had them.

Thirty-three cents in rejected nickels and pennies. He'd have called to the two women if they were in earshot, but they'd already gone out into the street. He slipped the coins into his jeans, thinking he might run into them later.

He always liked rolling up the coins he'd collected throughout month, pennies mostly, checking for old ones. Like the 1909-S VDB penny that was worth up to near $2,500 when last he looked it up.

The tellers, one in particular, the one with the thinning, black, permed hair, gave him the squint-eye look when he put the rolls down on the counter, and she pointed toward the coin machine.

The rolls, he felt, were solid. Substantial. They gave him a sense of self-worth in a way that was hard to explain and hard for him to come by. Dumping a plastic bag of coins in a machine was not the same. But he did it anyway.

At the teller's window, Jack handed the woman the slip from the machine like he was cashing in winning tickets at the track. Like when he'd go up to Saratoga each summer to watch the trotters with his uncle Fred before Fred moved to Palm Beach and turned to betting on the dogs.

He pocketed the seven dollars and fifty-seven cents, which was what was left after the bank took its cut. Where'd they get off doing that? Why'd he have to pay to use that machine that only made life easier for the tellers? Like Marie had said, someone's got to be making money off it, off *him*. There was seven ninety in his pocket now, counting the rejects tall Marie and the other woman had left.

At the Walgreen's, he waited while the clerk, a pretty girl with a long brown ponytail, went back to get his blood pressure pills. He looked over the Hershey's bars in boxes down below the counter. They cost a dollar nineteen each. In '55, they'd have cost no more than a nickel.

Jack had once taken his daughter and her friend to visit Hershey Park. Her twelfth birthday. The year after he and her mother had split. When he lost the house and he rented an apartment in a prewar building on the south shore.

The girls rode the spinning peanut butter cups, clutching each other, screaming, letting go of their adolescent guardedness for a few hours, then fell asleep together in the back seat on the way home.

His daughter had long since gone west. To Portland. She called him once a week. She was happy. She always said "Love you" before she hung up the phone. And he'd say, "Love you too."

He put two singles down on the counter for the copay. And when the girl turned away from the register, he picked up one of the chocolate bars and slipped it into his coat pocket. He hesitated a moment, counting the change again, and dropped the ninety cents he had on the counter.

"Have a good one," the girl called to him.

"You too!" he called back.

He sits there now at the kitchen table in afternoon sun, sipping the bitter coffee he heated up. The thin paper receipt and the string of useless coupons and the Hershey's bar are on the table in front of him. The folded five-dollar bill is there too. Five dollars is all that he has. Until next Wednesday when the Social Security check comes in the mail.

Money dogs him each day. To be true, it wears a person down. Saps everything out of you. But no excuse, though. Not for stealing. Even for only a few cents. He feels small for that. Worse than small. Worthless. A disappointment. For a piece of chocolate he didn't really need.

At Hershey Park, on that bright July day, money seemed no problem. He had a job. Thought he always would. Though what the "always" part really meant was never very clear to him. The meaning of "always" was too hard to seriously consider.

He would have given every penny he had then if it would make his daughter happy. He still would.

"Oh, Daddy," she said to him that day, "this is the best day of my whole entire life."

The Comforter of Sudden Souls

Harold Mandelbaum is a shomer. A watcher. A guardian of the dead. A comforter of sudden souls.

He is sitting on a thin cushion on the seat of a straight-backed wooden chair. The only chair in the room. A table lamp is lit in the corner near the chair. It provides only enough light so that he can read and allows him to dimly make out his surroundings. The walls of the room are painted in a brown shade of gray. A color that emanates solace. A color that absorbs sorrow.

There is no sound in the room beyond that of his own breathing, an occasional sigh, a clearing of his throat, the creak of the chair as he shifts his body against it. There is no window in the room. Only a door. And the door is shut.

He is not alone.

In the center of the room is a table, and on the table is the body of a man. Milton Hershkovitz is the man's name. A man of about seventy. A man unknown to Mandelbaum before he entered the room.

Mandelbaum, himself, is a man of seventy-three.

It is three in the morning. A Monday in May. An open book lies across Mandelbaum's knees. And from it he reads. He reads quietly to the man and to the man's soul.

He entered the room a few minutes after midnight and sat in the chair by the table with the body of Milton Hershkovitz on it. He relieved Seidman, the shomer who came before him. Seidman, a volunteer like Mandelbaum, nodded to him when he left. This is sacred work they do.

Hershkovitz had died in the late afternoon. His body had been washed and wrapped in a linen shroud. Kaplan had been the first watcher. Then Konigsberg. Then Seidman. Now Mandelbaum.

From the open book on his lap, Mandelbaum reads the Shema. "Shema Yisroel, Adonai elohenu, Adonai echod."

After death, it is said that a person must not be left alone. The shomer comes to sit with the body and to lend comfort to the attendant soul.

Mandelbaum feels a presence in the room. A stirring. A stirring in his mind.

What binds a soul to the body? What, then, releases the soul?

Mandelbaum believes that Hershkovitz's soul is close by the man's body. It is unsettled. Seeking peace. It will remain with the body until the body is buried. And then the soul is free to go. Until then, he, or another man, will sit with it. Be with it. Comfort it.

Yesterday morning, before Hershkovitz died, the soul had been Hershkovitz.

Is not the soul, in fact, the man we call Hershkovitz? Was it not the soul that suffered when Hershkovitz suffered? Was it not the soul that rejoiced when Hershkovitz rejoiced? Loved when Hershkovitz loved? Felt terror when Hershkovitz felt terror? What was Hershkovitz if not his soul? What or who could Hershkovitz have been without his soul?

What am I, then? thinks Mandelbaum. What more can I offer Hershkovitz now than to be in this room, at this time, with his soul? To sit with it. To ease the pain of separation. To mourn its loss. The loss it must feel.

Where will the soul go? Is it unsure? Does it not know how to leave or where to go? Is that the stirring I feel? Or is it my own disquieted soul I feel? Is my soul the teacher, or is mine the learner? Are some messages being passed between them?

Mandelbaum listens. He hears nothing. And so, he reads once more from the book of King David's Psalms.

"He maketh me to lie down in green pastures: he leadeth me beside the still waters. He restoreth my soul..."

He covers his eyes, sitting in the silence and the semidarkness. His feet find a more comfortable position. Other thoughts intrude. A dripping from the faucet in the bathroom?

He reads in a low voice from the Book of Job. "In the land of Uz, there lived a man whose name was Job. This man was blameless and upright; he feared God and shunned evil."

It is a story of anguish, of suffering, of sin and redemption, of transgression and forgiveness, of praise.

He pauses a moment in his reading. Did he hear something? He listens.

There is nothing to hear. Who is to speak in this room but me? Who is to listen? It is not for me that I read these psalms and verses. Is it not, then, for the listener without ears with which to hear? It is for the peace of the soul who resided within Hershkovitz and that is now waiting to be released.

His eyes tire. He rests. *This is allowed, Mandelbaum. Rest.* His eyes flutter and close. This rest is needed, allowed.

He is awakened by a stirring. A shiver. He opens his eyes, expecting Silverman to be at the door. But it is not time yet for Silverman to come.

He thinks he heard a voice. He knows he heard a voice. A voice not his own.

"Listen, Mandelbaum," the voice said, "don't kid yourself. You are reading to yourself. There is no one else here. You are doing a good thing. A mitzvah. This is true. But listen to the words carefully because, in truth, is it not to me, *your own soul,* you are speaking?"

He sits with the questions. What does he know of souls? What does anyone know?

Nothing.

"And after Job had prayed for his friends...all of his brothers and sisters and everyone who had known him before came and ate with him in his house. They comforted and consoled him..."

And then, after Mandelbaum finishes reading from the Book of Job, he hears a knock at the door. He opens it and lets Silverman come in.

As the two men pass each other in the doorway, each looks into the eyes of the other. They nod to each other. This is sacred work they do. And then Mandelbaum goes home.

They will call him again, he knows, another night, for another man, for another sudden, silent, hovering soul.

HANNAH AND MURRAY DISCUSS THE FUTURE

"Ma, where's Murray?"

"Out with Zeus."

"Murray names a dog *Zeus* and he gets away with it? Isn't that, like, sacrilegious or illegal or something?"

"Hannah, dear, it's only sacrilegious if someone first says, 'thou shalt not do that' or makes a law against it. Like, 'thou shalt not covet' or 'thou shalt not name a dog after a major or minor or even half-god of the universe,' for example."

"And could I do that?"

"Maybe. Ask your father."

"But what if I make a law like that and someone breaks it?"

"Well, Hannah, I guess it might depend upon several things, like who breaks it, or if they only break it once, or if a whole bunch of them break it, or if they break it by only thinking about it or just by planning to do it or not really meaning to do it, or if they do it sometimes while no one is watching, or if they do it and then apologize after but nobody believes their apology, or if—"

"Okay, Ma, thanks, I'll ask Dad."

"That's good, dear. He'll appreciate that since—"

"Dad, Ma said I should talk to you. It's about Murray."

"Have you spoken with Murray about the matter first?"

"Not exactly. Sort of, but not in those exact same words."

"Well, dear, it's disrespectful if you go over your brother's head

23

without speaking with him first, and so I suggest that you give some thought to possibly—"

"My God, no wonder nothing ever gets done around here anymore."

"What was that, dear?"

"Nothing, Dad."

"So, Murray, Dad said I should talk to you about something super really important."

"Did you leave a note in my in-box?"

"I tried, but it was full and not accepting any more messages, not since BC changed to AD or CE or whatever."

"Am I detecting a note of hostility and an incipient challenge to the established proto—"

"Cut the crap, Murray, I'm your sister. I need you to get in touch with Moses."

"Unfortunately, Hadassah—"

"Hannah."

"Unfortunately, Hannah, Moses passed on some time ago."

"Too bad. He was your front man, your mouthpiece, your homey with the commonfolk. And then you just drop him off at the edge of the Jordan like a day-old knish? Who'd you get to replace him?"

"Ah, good question. I'm still interviewing. I've had so little time to...I wish I had made better use of his skills. Sending him off into the desert was just a holding action until I—"

"You're shitting me, right?"

"I've had a few good prospects, but you know how hard it is finding—"

"I cannot goddamn believe this. You're telling me that you're okay with the way things are down there, with the floods and fires, polar ice melting, a million species of plants and animals gone which you made yourself all those zillions of years ago? And don't tell me you'll just make more when you have time and that it was only six days because we both know that's a crock because of the mutability of space-time continuum vectors, and you do nothing? Nada?"

"Nada?"

"Murray, are you even paying any attention? It's not like it was just an unpaid internship with Moses. He traipsed through the wilderness for forty years to find the promised land and when they got there, you told him you'd changed your mind and said no dice, folks, go back down the mountain, try again, and walk around for another thirty-eight years and then go attack the Amorites and, no worries, I'll have your back, so just massacre them and take their land. Are you kidding me? Then you did the same to the Reubinites, the Gadites, the Manassites, the meteorites, the stalactites and stalagmites, the Hittites, the Bagelbites, and all the others."

"You're mocking me, Hannah."

"And you sent them off smiting and wandering, meanwhile telling them don't worship the stars and the moon and the earth and the water and all the goddesses of creation, but they should obey only you, and about what they should wear, how many prayers to say how many times a day, and how not to eat anything nonkosher or non-halal. When soon there'll be no more shrimp or pigs to eat, anyway, Murray. I hope you took pictures of all the mountains and valleys and islands, giraffes, dinosaurs, pterosaurs, and *Euterpe precatoria* palms you made because you can say 'sayonara, baby' to it all unless you get off your skinny-ass butt and do something. Maybe you should have just let them go on worshipping the sky and the trees and the water in the first place. It couldn't have been any worse.

"Look, bro, you made up the 'eternal' thing. No one told you to say that. And so Moses kept calling you 'the Eternal.' He didn't call you the 'maybe-sometimes guy' or the 'just-for-a-little-while guy.' They counted on you. People believed everything you said. Have you looked at your firmament lately, by the way? Filled with satellites and pieces of satellites, used rocket parts, methane, Mylar balloons, dead insects, and microplastics.

"You wanted a monopoly. 'Have no gods before me.' You said that. And with me and Myron, and all the rest of us around. And Artemis, Aphrodite, Brahma the Creator, Vishnu the Preserver, Shiva the Destroyer, Buddha, and Gaia up here out of work…sure, we had our problems, but nothing like what's going on now. At least we answered the phone. But with you, who does anyone get when they call customer service? Face it, Murray, Deuteronomy may really have been the last chapter for you."

"Thank you, Hannah. I don't need your help, if that's what this is supposed to be. I'm not interested. I just figured I'd get them started and then, you know, let free will take them the rest of the way, right? That was the whole plan with the snake and the apple. Knowledge and free will. That was the deal. The plan."

"Murray, Murray. I get it now. The plan. Excellent! Knowledge, Free Will. Super! But what about Reason? What about Wisdom? Those would have been good to work in. But then you got way too involved. With the Commandments thing. Micromanagement. Look, it's either Free Will or it's not. I mean, after they ate the apple and put clothes on, you could maybe have dropped some hints about look out for the black plague or Styrofoam; or stay away from anything with the word *atomic* in it; or don't build houses downhill from Vesuvius; or avoid anyone with Stalin as a last name; or don't dig down any deeper than, say, ten cubits; and stay away from gun powder, bat caves, and people who won't wear a mask, for example, but not all those Commandments and 'thou shalts' and 'thou shalt nots.'"

"So what should I do now?"

"I had a little talk with Minerva. She's been through this before, and we think you need a new Moses type. Someone who doesn't have all the answers and all the rules. A mobilizer. Someone with creds. Experience. Charisma. Forward thinking. Sees the big picture. Team player. Works with their strengths. Gets them organized and then steps back."

"And that might be...who?"

"Now that you asked, Murray, you say the word and I'll set you up. I can get you in touch with this guy named LeBron. What have you got to lose?"

MALACHI AND HIS MOTHER
AT THE ALTSHUL ON GARFIELD PLACE

Malachi and his mother step into the side entrance of the shul. The tall mahogany front doors on 8th Avenue are closed. Locked tight. And so, the two of them walked around the corner and up Garfield and then up the stairs through the side entrance, then down the hallway to the sanctuary.

They take seats in one of the rear pews, passing by the Rothsteins, the Arbeiters, and the Edelmans seated in the front pews, the ones with the expensive ticket prices.

The room is near full. Everyone is masked. The hum of voices. Air conditioners whirring. The smell of aftershave and leather shoes.

"Why didn't Dad come with us?"

"Your father? He says he doesn't do gatherings anymore."

"COVID?"

"No. *Crabby.* He says he likes people well enough, but he likes them much better when he doesn't have to be around them."

"That's Bukowski."

"What?"

"Charles Bukowski, the poet, who said that about people."

"Don't tell your father. He thinks he made it up."

"It looks like the rabbi wants to start."

"Welcome all," the rabbi says, "I am Rabbi Plosker. Let us begin. We are all aware of the alarming increase in hate crimes and mass shootings. The Tree of Life Synagogue in Pittsburgh, the First

Baptist in Sutherland Springs, the Chabad of Poway, the AME in Charleston. And, friends, while we work against violence of all kinds, visited upon people of all faiths, we must also protect ourselves with guards, and vigilance, and yes, with preparedness."

Malachi's mother's face is flushed. "I have to get up," she says.

"Ma, wait. It's starting."

"I have to leave."

"Why? I'll go with you."

"No, you stay. I thought I could do this, but I can't. I have to go. I cannot be here for this. All these people. The police."

She gets up, clutching her purse, and walks toward the side door, the way they came in. A police officer is there. She turns back up the center aisle toward the main entrance.

"Ma'am," the officer there tells her, "I'm sorry, but you can't leave."

"I have to. You can't stop me."

"Ma'am." The officer extends his arm and takes a step to obstruct her way. "Please, ma'am. We have a protocol we need to follow, and I ask you to cooperate, for the benefit of all."

"Malachi!"

"I'm sorry, ma'am, you have to go back to your seat." He touches her elbow and points her back down the aisle.

She sits down. She's shaking. "Malachi, please say something. Look what is happening here."

"Ma, it will be okay. Nothing's happening. Trust me. Look, the rabbi wants to begin."

"The rabbi? She wants to begin now? She wants to begin with the gestapo barring the doors?"

"What are you saying? The police do these trainings all over the city. In mosques, churches, synagogues. It's for our own safety. We need to know what to do if, God forbid, something happens, if someone with a gun comes in."

"Open your eyes, Malachi. The 'someone with a gun' is already here. There are two someones with guns here. One is at the front door and the other is at the side door, and Plosker herself invited them in. She invited them in, yet. With guns, yet. Tell me, who comes into synagogue with a gun? I'll tell you who. My dead grandmother knows the answer in her grave. The SS, that's who."

"Everyone is watching us, Ma."

"Yes, they're watching. With their goddamn eyes closed. They're watching but not seeing. This is the most *farshtunkene* idea I have ever heard in my life and, you, my own son, brought me here."

"Shhh!"

The officer at the back of the sanctuary is holding an air horn, a large orange Klaxon. He's wearing sunglasses, a dark uniform, a peaked cap, epaulets, and a COVID mask. He nods. Touches his visor with two easy fingers.

"Sergeant Petersen here," the rabbi says, pointing to the officer in the rear, "will lead us through a training in an active shooter drill. He will show us what to do in the very, very remote possibility of an active shooter coming into the sanctuary, God forbid. If we are prepared, and we act quickly and with intention and preparation, we can save our lives. The lives of all of us."

"That's right," says Petersen. "We're here to help keep you as safe as possible. I promise you, no one will be hurt. We ask you first to turn your phones off." He waits. Everyone fumbles with their phones. "In a few moments, when you hear the sound of the horn..."

"Malachi, take me out of here. I can't do this. I will have a heart attack. I can't. I can't...I will die in this room."

"...and as soon as you hear it, I want you to immediately do whatever you would do if an active shooter came into the room."

Sgt. Petersen steps back out of the sanctuary and closes the doors behind him. The officer at the side entrance does the same.

A long moment of silence passes. The doors open. Both police officers, wearing masks, both with the Klaxon horns pointed at the pews, step in.

Blam! Blam! Blam! The horns crack open the air. Again and again and again like a pair of monstrous screaming jackhammers.

A woman in the rear screams. Three men in the front row stand up and look to the back, then to the front, toward the blaring sounds. The rest stand, look around, and then duck under the pews, covering their heads and pulling the others down with them. Some grab for their phones.

Malachi pulls at his mother's skirt. "Mama, get down here."

The cracking, blasting sounds stop. There are cries from all sides.

Petersen, holding the Klaxon in his hand like a handgun, walks down the aisle, pointing with it from one side to the other, pointing at each one of the half-hidden, half-crouching, cowering people.

"You're dead! You're dead, you're dead," he says to each of them as he looks at them.

The officer at the side door explains, "The worst thing you can do is to stand up and look at the shooter, giving him a target. The next worst thing is to crouch under the pews. You make yourself a stationary target. A dead one."

"You're all dead. Every one of you. Figuratively," says Petersen. "Now let's try it one more time."

The two officers step behind the doors again.

"See, Ma?"

"See what? They told us nothing about how we should react," she says. She stands up. "Listen to me. This is their new trick," she yells to everyone.

"Please sit down."

"Yes, please sit down," the rabbi calls out.

"That was a sham! One crazy kid bursting through the door like Dylann Roof or Gregory Bowers doesn't kill enough of us? What they had was just old-school hatred. This is the new and improved US version of mass killing."

"Someone, take her out of here," says Rothstein.

"They're not going to let me out of here. Not you either, Rothstein. Not peacefully. They have us where they want us. They have us all trapped, totally lulled into fearful, willing, trusting fools, placated, convinced they mean no harm. Like how they convinced my grandparents to wait in line for the boxcars, carrying their suitcases and children, and then in line at the showers, for godsake. I know what's coming. Everyone get out. Now. All of us, all at once. Make a run for it. Rush them. I swear, our only hope is to take them by surprise. Because the next time those two doors open, they'll have AR15s and..."

The Aftermath of the
Incident at the Altshul

"Mel Rothstein called me this morning. He had this clenched-throat anger in his voice. Like he was trying to stuff it back down. Showing me how in control he was."

Malachi sits across from his mother at the kitchen table. She spilled some sugar as she was adding more of it to her coffee. She pushes the crystals around on the slick tablecloth with her finger as she speaks.

"What did he say to you?" Malachi asks.

"He said, 'How could you?' He said I had fomented an insurrection. An armed insurrection. At the temple. The 'temple,' he called it. He said I had ruined the reputation of the whole congregation he had worked so hard to make and that tweets or posts or whatever they call them had been posted across the Internet. Pictures of me. Rage on my face. Leading a mob of radical Jews against the police. Calling them Nazis. Threatening them."

"I saw the pictures."

"He said that he had expected more from me, which I know is a lie because he has never expected anything from me, or any other woman, beyond dullness, muteness, subservience, and a look of thankful awe."

She presses her finger into the mound of sugar she created and puts what has stuck to her finger into her mouth. Her lower lip curls up. Her chin wrinkles. She begins to cry. Malachi reaches across the table toward her.

"I feel so terrible," she says. "I'm glad your father wasn't there. I don't know what he would have done."

"Ma, I feel so bad for you. I know you meant well. In the most genuine, human sense, you saw a danger and you wanted to save everyone. You weren't crying wolf or 'fire' in a theater. You thought those cops were real terrorists intent on shooting everyone in the room and that the whole congregation was sitting like obedient sheep waiting for the doors to open and the shooting to start."

"That's what Rothstein called me. A terrorist. Worse than a terrorist, he said. He said I should be ashamed of myself for risking everyone's lives for my own neurotic *mishigas*. He said I needed to get help."

"Ma, Rothstein himself ran out. I saw him. He ran out without looking back, without offering to help anyone. He burst through the side door. He knocked down the officer there. He ran out of the building the second he heard you scream 'Get out!' It's only now that he feels embarrassed. He shouldn't feel embarrassed. He did the right thing. You did the right thing. They had guns. They were acting like real active shooters. They meant to scare the shit out of us. Out of everyone. And, I may be wrong, but I think they got some sort of charge out of scaring the shit out a bunch of cornered Jews."

"Rothstein. I never liked him. But that's totally separate, Malachi. For the first time in my life, I feared for my own mortality. Not in the philosophical sense. Not just in a conversation over cocktails. Not in that casual, intellectual sense of 'let's all talk about death' in some abstract, manageable way. But in the real gripping fear of death in that very moment. Certain that I'd be shot and killed. Ripped through with bullets, and that my body, me, my mind, my thoughts, my very self, would be lost. Gone. Lost to consciousness. Lost to all reality, to all eternity. It is a fear unlike any other human feeling. That instant awareness of imminent death."

"I can only begin to imagine how you felt, Ma. When I was twelve or thirteen, at night, in bed, I would think of the vastness of the universe or infinity. The blankness. The unending black void. I could feel my body imploding, crushing in upon itself with fear. The fear of nothingness."

"I don't remember that. Why didn't you tell me?"

"I wanted to. I'd get out of bed in the middle of the night like I needed to escape my own thoughts as though they were a physical being. As if death and nothingness were physical beings. Even though it's the total lack of physicality of them that is really the most incomprehensible and frightening of all. I needed to get out. Just like you did. I left my room, and I went to your bedroom door. It was closed, and I didn't knock."

"You should have, Malachi, that's what parents are for."

"It's not that I didn't want to wake you. It's that I didn't want to frighten you."

"Frighten me?"

"I thought that talking about death with you, so much older than me and so much closer to death, would bring up those same fears for you. So I just sat there until I felt I should go back to bed."

"I'm so sorry."

"That's when I started saying a prayer at night."

"What kind of prayer? I never taught you prayers."

"The one with 'Our father, who art in heaven.' The one with 'give us this day our daily bread' and 'the valley of the shadow of death.' 'Forgive us our trespasses.' I didn't know if it was a real prayer. It just made me feel better to say those things. And I'd say 'Bless my mother and father' and list all the people who I wanted to protect and say it in exactly the right order or I'd have to start all over again to say it right, no matter how many times. And then there was one night when I was going to bed and instead of 'Good night, see you in the *morgen*—like *guten morgen*—like I would say every night, I said 'see you in the *morgue*.' And my God, I apologized a hundred times and then I cried and cried and all I could think of was that what I had said would really make that happen and that you'd die because I said that."

"Malachi, I'm so sorry."

"Don't be sorry, Ma. And don't be sorry for doing what you thought was right and good, no matter how it turned out. And forget about Rothstein. He's not thinking of you, only himself."

They looked at each other. Eye to eye.

"My coffee is cold, and I spilled sugar all over the table. Sit, I'll make us fresh. And let's talk about something else."

"Critical race theory?"

"Oh, yeah, that's a good one. You should hear what your aunt Frieda has to say about that. Like she might even know what it means."

BREAKING THE JUDY BLUE EYES RULE

Nathan M. flew from Boston's Logan to West Palm. He had taken a few days off from work. His oldest son picked him up at the airport and they talked on the ride up to St. Lucie. Mostly about the weather, their jobs, and the Mets. It was during spring training season, and it felt to Nathan just like a late July afternoon in the Back Bay.

Nathan asked if he could turn up the car radio. *Piano Man* was playing.

His son always had Billy Joel on whenever he picked Nathan up in his truck. He wondered whether his son really liked Billy Joel or if he only played it because they used to listen to him, with the volume turned high, when the two of them lived together. That was in the years after Nathan and his mother had split and his son had moved back home after college. Either way, it made Nathan happy. He felt his shoulders relax.

His son had started calling him regularly after his mother had been diagnosed with ALS. This was after he'd finished grad school and had gotten married to a young woman from Mississippi, and they moved to Florida to be near to his mother.

Nathan and Helen had three children and all three moved to Florida to be near her. By then, Nathan had remarried and had two young children with his new wife. They lived in Boston, close to where her family was.

Each of his older children and their partners were in Helen's downstairs bedroom with the hospital bed, a couple of chairs, and pieces of medical equipment. No one spoke when he walked in. They all looked at him and smiled. He and Helen had had a troubled past.

They all took turns sitting briefly in the chair beside Helen's bed. The IV drip had been unplugged, though the line with the morphine pump was still clicking on and off. Nathan sat by the bed once for a few minutes, hoping and not hoping she would open her eyes and see him there. A thin blanket covered her body. Her face was sharp and gaunt.

He and Helen had married in August of '66. It had been hot. He'd worn a suit he'd rented and Helen wore her grandmother's wedding dress.

In the one picture Nathan kept of Helen, the first one he had ever taken of her, on one of the first days they'd spent together, she's standing beside his car in three-quarter profile, one skeptical eyebrow raised. Her hand shading her eyes from the sun. She's wearing a light-colored summer dress. The photo was from September '65. A little less than a year before they were married.

After Nathan had been in the room for a while, the hospice nurse came in to say, "Sometimes, right near the end, you see, one or another of you might consider leaving the room, just so you can ease the passing."

She'd said it to all of them, but he was the only one who left.

He went out for a walk, passing by pastel condos much the same as hers. Neat lawns. Palm trees. Swept driveways. Clean white cars with Michigan, Ontario, and Sunshine State licenses. Nobody to be seen in the yards. No sounds other than those of yelping poodles behind closed doors and trucks on the Interstate.

In the ten months before he and Helen were married, they had taken short, uncomplicated trips. Eating pizzas with garlic and onion in places they'd never been before, sharing a Coke with no ice. Finishing the whole pie right there in the booth, wiping the grease off their chins and fingers, laughing, and rating the pizza half-seriously for the quality of its crust, chew, sauce, cheese, and its New York-style foldability. Tony and Tina's on Arthur Avenue, Joe's on Carmine Street, Patsy's on 56th. The Famous and not so Famous Original Rays. Patsy Grimaldi's on Front Street.

Driving around with the windows open playing Zombies and Stones tapes. Cramming for organic chemistry together, memorizing the hydrohalogenation reaction of an asymmetric alkene or the Bischler-Napieralski reaction. He wanted badly to go to medical school. She wasn't interested in any more school and wanted to get a job. He got a D in Organic.

So, instead, they got married.

Before that, in June or July, Nathan told his older brother that he couldn't do it. Couldn't go through with it. "No way," he said. He was twenty-one. Scared. Not at all what he wanted. His brother said if that was a legit reason for not getting married, nobody would do it. "You need a better excuse than that," he said. "If that's your only reason, it's not good enough."

It was during that part of the sixties that still hung on tightly to the norms of the fifties. Pre-Woodstock. Pre-sexual revolution. Pre-EST. Pre-consciousness-raising. The pre-let's-see-the-world-for-a-while-before-we-just-rush-into-something-stupid part of the sixties.

His brother said their mother would throw a shitfit if he backed out.

They moved into an apartment together, bought an Ethan Allen couch and a rocking chair, taped pictures up on the walls, and kept their socks and underwear in separate dressers.

Neither of them knew anything about marriage, at least not good ones. They followed the hand-me-down script they were given, with nothing more to go on. Nothing that might help them avert twenty years of quiet unhappiness, depression, anxiety, resentment, isolation, muddled affairs, and bone weariness. No real, deep understanding of love to guide them.

Both of them, wanting, expecting, to love and to be loved. They didn't know how to make that happen and didn't see a way out, as if they both kept stepping across a muddy river that only seemed to get wider and deeper the further they got in.

They were little more than adolescents dressed up to look like adults, wrapped in the thin-at-the-elbows neuroses their parents had given to them. They were no good together, and each was too afraid to say it.

They split, and found they were so much better apart. Separately happier. It just took so long for that to happen.

She died that afternoon while he was out walking.

Then, as she lay, so recently alive, so recently herself, all of that past came welling up in him.

And so he cried. For her. For the sadness of it all. For the kids.

On the flight back up to Logan, looking down at the blue, blue ocean, he listened to the circling lyrics of songs he once knew by heart and now only remembered in fragments on repeat in his brain. Words and melodies worn deeply into the grooves of his synapses. *Suite: Judy Blue Eyes.*

Only then, as the words came to him, did he finally understand the Judy Blue Eye's rule. What Crosby, Stills & Nash's lyrics had meant: that you should not let thinking of the past keep you from seeing the reality of present.

He had stood by her bed. Taken his turn in the chair beside her. And, even then, in those moments when she had so little time left, he still didn't see her as who she was. Only as who she had been… and only in relation to himself, as he had done for so long, seeing her only clouded by the remnants of who she had seemed to him to be in the past. Not the woman she was, or who she always had been.

Reading the Letter
from Birmingham City Jail

Lester doesn't write me anymore. He used to. Once a week. It's been six months since the last one. I wait each day for a letter from him. I know better than to hope for one, but I do.

He writes well. He works at it. He puts his heart in it. His soul. Truly, his soul. He curates his words. Looks for the right one. Or, if needed, conjures up one himself. So few of us feel we have the permission to make up words. He does that. I've never tried.

I love him.

I don't know where he is.

We read Martin Luther King Jr.'s "Letter from Birmingham City Jail" together. All of us. Nine men. Eight of them black, one white. And me. I am a white woman. I teach writing. I work in correctional facilities. That's where the work is. Rikers Island. Edgecombe. Queensboro. Mostly at Rikers.

In class one afternoon, soon after I started teaching there, in the group, he said, "What is a word, anyway? A representation, right? Only a sound. With a meaning you give to it. A meaning you get from it. Something we agree upon."

Another man turned to him and said something I didn't understand. And then he pretty much kept his mouth shut after that. I could see what life was like for him. Bruising.

The next day, he wrote me a letter. I'd given them cards with my name and address, so I wasn't surprised that he wrote. He's the only one who did. Of the nine men, he was the only one who wrote. It was a letter-writing class.

He signed the letter 'Lester.' He used the single quote marks. I wrote back.

After that, we wrote to each other once a week, even after the class ended.

None of the men were yet alive in 1963 when King wrote his letter. None of them had read it before. Some had heard about it, they said.

My husband, at the time, thought teaching the letter was a bad idea. "You'll stir them up," he said.

Of course it'll stir them up. That was part of the point. The other part of the point was the language. Each of King's impassioned thoughts leading to the next. Torment, outrage, love, and courage buttressing one another in every paragraph. A letter like that is not a cover letter for a job application. It's the manifesto of a movement. Of course, it will stir them up. It should stir up *everyone* up.

We read the first five paragraphs the first day. Each person read aloud a few sentences and then on around the circle. We talked about the words. Unfamiliar ones. Ones that held the most power. Purposeful words. Simple. Direct. Unflinching words.

They asked, who was King writing to? Why is it six pages long? We took four weeks to read the whole letter.

By the end of the fourth week, Lester wrote that he felt his life had been changed by reading it.

He thought about me each day, he wrote.

The issue of nonviolence was approached with care. Did King make a good case for it? Was he just being naïve? Was he inviting harm to others? How could he expect men, women, and children to stand still and take a blow or a bullet or a mauling by a dog? How does nonviolence apply to each of us? Can you be nonviolent in Rikers? Do you feel like King in any way? Unfairly and prejudicially treated by a hostile system? An agent of change?

They talked about Attica. White supremacy. Incarceration. Reparations. All of that. John Lewis. Malcolm. Bobby Seale. After each class, they wrote a letter about something that came up for them.

We read Woolf's *A Room of One's Own*. Woolf's words were transcendent. We read Frederick Douglass's "What to the Slave is the Fourth of July?"

They read. Faithfully. They wrote. Letters to family. Girlfriends. Cuomo. Newspapers. Thoughtful letters. Filled with a clear and well-tempered passion.

The more I saw him, the more I came to need to be with him.

I wrote a letter to the judge for him. My husband told me I'd used bad judgment. That I was going too far. "What is too far?" I said.

"This is," he said.

We read Celie's letters in *The Color Purple*.

"I'm only trying to help him."

"Let his mother help him."

"I have the resources his mother may not have."

"My God, listen to yourself! You're not the mother to the world. You have your own two kids. Think of them."

"Exactly. I am. Wouldn't I want someone to do for them what I'm doing for another mother's child? Would you not want that for them?"

"But my children will not be in jail. They won't hold up a grocery store."

"How do you know that? How can you say that with such walled-off, self-centered surety? We could be one terrible mistake away from that. Would you want your child to spend one night in jail, much less five or ten years? What or who would they be when they came out? This man is asking for help and I'm helping him."

"You're being duped. Used. Face it. Grow up. There's a big, hard reality out there that you can't seem to get—'you do the crime, you do the time.'"

"No, you're the one being duped," I told him. "Your 'I-know-it-all, I've-done-it-all-on-my-own,' self-made-man bullshit you tell yourself. Eighty-five percent of people in Rikers have not been convicted of a crime. That's eight thousand men and women behind bars. Eight thousand. And they're in that hellhole because they couldn't make pretrial bail. They're *not* criminals."

"They really have you by the short hairs, don't they? This homey saw a bleeding-heart liberal walk in the door holding a 'Get Out of Jail Free' card, and you're it. You planning on paying his bail?"

"Fuck you."

"No, fuck you."

We wrote back and forth for almost a year. A few friends helped me put up bail for him.

By that time, my husband was tired of sleeping in the basement and he moved out.

Lester needed a place to stay, and he moved in. The kids were pretty okay with that. But nobody else was. I mean *nobody*.

Then my husband took the kids from me.

Lester and I said we could make it. We'd find a way.

We did.

And then we didn't.

He needed to go, he said. He said he'd write. Tell me where he was. Told me that sometimes you define yourself by how other people see you. And then by who you were at another time or place. But then, it's only who you are in relation to who you need to be that matters. He thanked me, and then he left.

He's right, of course. He needed to go. And I'll make it, I know. Somehow. I still write to him. It helps me make sense of things. To make peace with myself. I may mail the letters if he sends me his new address.

Two Men on a Bench
by the Water Looking East

"No time to be homeless, is it?"

"No, sir."

"Not a good time at all. There's good times and good places, but not here and not now."

"No, sir."

"Name's Richard."

"Jack."

"Nice to meet you, Jack."

"You too, Richard."

"You got it? A lot of people do, you know. You gotta watch out. Be careful as shit."

"Don't believe so."

"Me neither. You never know, though. They say you could have it and not feel sick."

"I heard that."

"A lot of guys, they have it, don't tell anyone, then get a bed for the night some place and next thing you know everybody else has it. Better to be out on your own, like us, I say. The only safe place, you know. You sure about not having it?"

"Yes, pretty sure, mostly."

"I'll sit over here, though. Keep a stretch of the bench between us. Keep looking out at the water. I don't mean to cast no aspersions, you know. Just being sure, you know. I don't mean no offense."

"I understand. None taken."

"Where you from, Jack?"

"Boston."

"Why'd you come way up to this winter shithole? Nights get cold as a dead man's dick here. Not cold as Albany, for sure. That's where I'm from. Albany. Why'd you come here, again?"

"No place else to go. Got some family here. Williston. I took the train out."

"They won't take you in?"

"Maybe. I don't know."

"I got ya. Any kids, Jack?"

"No."

"Three for me. Old. Out on their own. A long time since I seen them. Like to some time. 'Fore I die,' I like to say. What's in the bag?"

"Water bottle. Sliced cheese. Wipes. Phone. Charger. Earbuds. A book. Two. A loaf of bread I squeezed down flat. Pair of socks. Toothbrush. Twizzlers. That's pretty much it."

"Shit, Jack. That's a well-planned stash. I shoulda had you pack one for me. Not that I need anything I can't find on my own. You got a place to sleep? Me, I got a few places. Regular ones. You look around. See who's home. Who's not."

"Don't know yet. Shelter, maybe."

"The shelter? Fuck no, Jack. Find a place by yourself. Get off the streets. Cops looking. Wherever you go, scoot if somebody else shows up. Keep your pack on you. Some guys aren't so friendly. But find a place out of the wind. Wind's the killer. Reminds me, you ever read *Ironweed*? William Kennedy? Great book. About Albany. A guy named Phelan. Francis, I think. Kennedy nails him. A bum like me. Thinks a lot. Drinks a lot. Has a friend, name of Helen. She freezes to death one night. They find her the next day in a doorway. Breaks Francis up. Won a Pulitzer. Albany's no place to be in the winter."

"Never read it. It sounds grim."

"What's not grim now, Jack?"

"Some things. The water's nice out there. The sun out there on the water. The way the gray waves curl over, white on top, with that light blue-green underneath."

"I'll give you that. The waves. The sound they make. Nice. You ever been out to LA, Jack?"

"Once."

"Waves out there. They swell up like a humpback rising, and they fall all of a sudden. You feel it thud in your chest like your own heart's a drum. Damn! You can sit on the beach there all night. See the sun go down all red and pink and purple and the stars come out. The sky gets so dark it grabs the light right out of your eyes and pulls it away from you like a sudden gust of wind in your face pulls the breath out of your lungs. God, I wish I was there."

"Me too."

"Nights like that make you think about all the things you don't know and won't ever. Nobody will. All the thoughts people had once, like Jesus, and Einstein, and your grandmother, and her grandmother, and how all their electrical brain energy might've gotten caught up in like an asteroid belt circling over us all the time. And maybe some of the energy gets caught in the gravity and gets attached to the rain and falls down on all of us randomly. Like when you sit alone sometimes and you think things you never thought before."

"I never thought about it like that so much."

"Times like these make you think things like that. Like all the people dying now, their brains firing away a mile a minute and hundreds of thousands, millions, of thoughts and wishes. And all the fear washing away from them, and they have that last peaceful thought when they pass. The air is filled with all of them moving through walls and trees and into us. Each of us thinking Chinese thoughts and Italian thoughts, old man thoughts, little baby thoughts. Thoughts we need to pay attention to. Open our brains to, you know."

"I guess."

"Look at me, Jack. I don't know you from a hole in a ham sandwich, but you seem like a fish out of a tank here, and you know what happens to them. I seen guys like you, and I'm telling you straight. They don't make it. You have options. Maybe I do, too, but this is my life now. I may not make it, either, but this is all's I know, and I'm not changing. So you call your wife or your mother or whoever. Tell them the truth. Tell yourself the truth. They'll set you up, man. Guaranteed. They're family. This ain't the answer. They are."

"I don't know."

"I do. All's I'm sayin' is give yourself a chance, man, while you still got one....Now listen up, Jack, hear those voices. Do what's right for you and everyone else. And take this mask I got here, put it on your face, go get tested, and take your fucking Halloween goody bag there and get the fuck off my fucking bench."

UNCERTAIN TIMES

Several days ago, I was preparing to move from a large high-ceilinged loft in the West Village in which I'd been living with a good friend I'd met in graduate school years ago, and into a tiny one-bedroom space on Hester Street, across town on the Lower East Side.

Rune, my friend, had abruptly decided to move back to Chicago to be closer to his father, given that Rune's mother had died suddenly. She had been fine up until only a few days before her death. A healthy and robust woman of short stature, high resilience, and an indomitable spirit, she had the steel-plated bearing of a person who, early in her life in Kyoto, had endured deep hardship and constant uncertainty. She'd been raised by her mother after her father died late in the war with the Allies, leaving them destitute with no apparent means of support and with only their desire to survive.

I couldn't afford to purchase the loft, and Rune needed to sell it.

Though it was a surprising turn of events, I understood and appreciated the circumstances. I came to see the opportunity as a welcome change of environment.

In the midst of watching the inauguration, I sorted through cardboard boxes stuffed with research notebooks, manuscript drafts, and reprints of journal articles I'd accumulated over the years, items that should have been tossed long ago. I also came across a scientific paper presented at the 6th International Conference on Agents and Artificial Intelligence in 2014, which Rune and I had attended together in the city of Angers, in the west of France.

Rune, being a member of the society, had brought me along as a guest, though I, a biologist, had only the most rudimentary understanding of the theoretical underpinnings of AI. The paper was titled "Quantum Probability and Operant Conditioning: Behavioral Uncertainty in Reinforcement Learning," and I had no recollection of why I had felt the need to bring it back to the states and then to file it among my other papers, though it was likely a tangible reminder of our time together.

I sat on the hardwood floor of the loft. Warm midafternoon light streamed in through the floor-to-ceiling windows as I read through the article.

For no reason I can identify, as I read the paper, I experienced a growing consciousness of a post-inaugural mental and emotional reset beginning to wash over me. It was akin to slowly immersing myself in a warm bath or to feeling the soothing, unexpected touch of a long-lost lover. I had a growing sense of distancing myself from the ragged, rageful, and disorienting last four years of the Trump administration, though it had been only a few hours since I had watched the surprisingly peaceful transition to the new president's administration.

The constant tension I had been gripped with during those years was dissipating. The reflexive need to check my email and the constantly breaking news feeds was no longer vexingly immediate. My ability to focus my attention on the details in the paper grew, and I became caught up in a discourse on behavioral positive-negative basis vectors in quantum state space. I found that the difficult concepts applicable to human and AI responses to uncertainty began to flow through my mind as easily as clear water in an unimpeded woodland stream at the start of a spring thaw.

Whether or not the former president and his witting and unwitting enablers had planned the relentless perpetration of shape-shifting uncertainty and disruption we endured over the last four years, I saw clearly in this short theoretical paper a reasonable explanation of the social, economic, psychological, and political angst in which we had all been caught and, perhaps also, a way forward.

In short, the authors presented a cogent argument, based solidly on the dynamics of ψ wave function in quantum mechanics, for the way in which the behavior of systems as widely different as stock market movement, political opinion, and human behavior operate when the degree of uncertainty increases beyond an experiential norm—namely, when the degree of randomness and unpredictability of a system feedback either strays or is pushed beyond the limits to which the system was designed to operate, and for which there is neither a homeostatic nor a stochastic mechanism for the maintenance of a system stability.

We all expect a degree of randomness in our lives, a certain degree of unpredictability that we learn to live with and accept as normal. AI systems, too, accept and learn from unexpected responses and build them into their database. Algorithms are designed to incorporate a level of unpredictability. For example, a rat can adapt to being unsure of a reward or punishment for a while, but when the unpredictability frequency goes beyond a certain degree of expectation, it loses interest and no longer pays attention. It becomes unpredictable itself—apathetic at one moment and violently aggressive at the slightest perceived provocation at another. It has lost its sense of control. It becomes berserk. Its life is disrupted. It becomes asocial. Sociopathic.

I set the paper aside, and in that moment, I was struck by the confluence of the many seemingly random and unpredictable events that had recently entered my life: the death of my dear friend's mother; his impending move from the city; my need to move to a new and unfamiliar location and the possible risk of exposure to infection during the move; uncertainty of when, if ever, I would qualify for the COVID vaccine; the waxing and waning fear that the city would be beset by groups of rioters bent on disruption following the inauguration; the realization that my financial situation would change with an increase in my rent; and the depressingly uncertain economy. All this, along with the unexpected, pleasant memory of a past time spent with Rune, was brought to me by a scientific paper whose language I could only barely grasp but the meaning of which I felt, in a way, had been transformational.

Yeats was wrong. I saw that neither the system, nor I, had failed. The center held. Neither it nor I had exceeded the limits of our ability to recover, and a young woman with a radiant mind had spoken with a wisdom that we, and the system, had been aching to hear.

THE END OF THE ROLL

Bessie Levin waited to see the manager.

"How may I help you, ma'am?" he said. He was well-groomed, polite, and had "Bernard Sopotnick" stitched on the pocket of his red Costco vest.

There were nine Costco stores within a one-hundred-mile radius of Bessie's apartment in Bensonhurst. She had spoken in-person, face-to-face, with the store manager of eight of them. She had gotten nowhere with any of them. You name them: Sunset Park, Elmhurst, Staten Island, Bayonne. Nothing.

The last one on her list, and the one in which Bernard Sopotnick was standing before her, was on Krocks Road in Allentown, Pennsylvania.

She arrived at 7:30 a.m. The line at the entrance was sparse. Things looked promising here, she thought, 97.3 miles from her home in the epicenter of big-box, high-stakes, competitive consumerism.

The congenial woman ahead of her in line shared that she was just there for eggs, lactose-free milk, Double Stuf Oreos—for her three little Biedermans—Purell, and a sixteen-pack of Charmin. "What are you here for?" she asked Bessie.

"Oh, you know, milk, eggs, bread, Tums, the basics."

Bessie generally abjured lying, even to complete strangers. Today was different. Today was like the last lightning round of *Supermarket Sweep* meets Final Jeopardy.

55

She had memorized the floor plan of every Costco in the Northeast. The doors opened at 10:00.

Not stopping for a cart or the free samples of radish kimchi or vegan bacon mac and cheese, Bessie darted to aisle D 13, bypassing the milk, eggs, and bread (that was only a ploy) as fast as her Hush Puppies Power Walkers could take her.

A small crowd had already formed in the aisle. There were women milling around with surgical masks on and men watching, wearing their masks under their chins. All were staring at a six-inch-high block-lettered sign: "We are sold out of water, bath tissue, and paper towels. We are sorry for any inconvenience."

Inconvenience? Are you goddamn kidding me? Inconvenience? she thought. Inconvenience is when you miss your bus. Inconvenience is forgetting to pack your Dentu-Creme. This was no inconvenience. This was the outer limit of habitable life. This was the end of the line for Bess.

"Sir," she said sweetly to Sopotnick. "Would you be a dear and get me a package of toilet paper?"

"Sold out."

"I know," she said. "I read the sign, but could you just check again for me?"

"Trust me, ma'am, we sold the last 96-pack last night."

"Sir," she said, showing him her card, "I have been a member since 1996. Please check just one more time for me. I'll wait."

"Ma'am..."

She'd already run the list of BJ's, Best Buy, Walmart, and Target. All "temporarily out of stock." What does "temporarily" mean to a woman on the edge?

How long is "temporarily" when you've blown through every roll of Scott and Cottonelle toilet paper, every existing dinner napkin and Kleenex, every brown take-out order napkin and even the take-out bags themselves, as well as all the little paper receipts in the apartment?

When you've filched every roll from Starbucks, Dunkin' Donuts, and Arby's you could. When your cheeks are raw from using every last page of the *New York Times* and the *New Yorker* in sight. And even when it goes against every shred of urbane civility you think you have and you use the torn pages of *People, Us Weekly,* and *The National Inquirer* from your neighbors' recycling bins. *What,* she wondered, *is the utilitarian meaning of "temporarily"?*

She had searched online, Googling *toilet paper, bath tissue, baby wipes.* Sure, she could find plenty of toy skid-shot toilet-paper blaster guns and free shipping deals on rapid-fire sheet-storm toilet-paper blaster guns (along with one free starter roll), which, according to Amazon, "other customers like her" had also searched for. But just plain, no-frills, unquilted, two-ply toilet paper? Sold out. Single-ply? Sold out.

"Listen to me, boychik, I am not known to be an angry person, and I am asking you politely, one human being to another, forget that I am a loyal customer and you're a store manager, forget that I am old enough to be your grandmother, or I could be a distant 23andMe cousin of your own grandmother, but forget all that. Forget everything except that you are a good person, and I am a good person, and I am in need, and you have what I need, and good things happen to people like you who do good things for people like me. And like the Bible says, do unto others, you know, so I am asking you one last time, in the abundant goodness of your heart, that while you go get a footlong dog and a Big Gulp with this twenty I am slipping into your manager's jacket pocket, you unlock the employee storeroom and I'll slit open the glacier-size stack of Kirkland ass wipes we both know is in there somewhere with a box cutter I will borrow from the first associate I see, and I'll grab two rolls, two rolls only, and make my way out through the 'No Exit' exit before Lothar in security, who is probably right now sitting on the crapper himself because he has run out of bath tissue at home, is any the wiser, and I will be on my way. No harm done.

Not a single word spoken. You will have done your civic duty for the fast-vanishing proverbial Common Good, and one day, God willing, I will meet you in heaven and I'll save a good table for you, and we will talk about all of this and laugh out loud. So how about it, Bernard?"

"Ma'am..."

"Don't 'ma'am' me, Bernie. Let's you and me walk over to 'Employees Only' right now and if there are no rolls in there, I will go quietly. If there are, then you give me two, you keep the twenty I gave you, and I am out of here. But if you refuse to open the door, I'll know why, and I will head over to Toys and Games and hand out an armload of those rapid-fire toilet-paper sheet-storm blaster guns, and we will start a little goddamn toilet paper revolution. Capiche, Bernie?

On Considering Quotidian Days

A thunderstorm passed over the island last night. We counted the seconds between the flash of lightning and the thunder, as if that would have any effect on us. How fast the storm was moving mattered none to us. We were going nowhere. We had closed all the windows. The wind was stiff and strong. We didn't lose power.

The next morning, Peter is in his study cleaning the cat's litter box.

"Would you like some coffee?" I ask.

"Yes," he says.

We sit and have coffee together. We do this most mornings now, talking about what we have to do today. Our lists. He writes his on index cards. He carries them in his back pocket along with a pen. He writes notes to himself. Ideas for the stories he writes. The last time we were in the city, he bought a box of the pens he likes. A box lasts him years.

That was before COVID. We haven't been back there since before last March. He says we probably won't get there again for maybe another year or two.

"A year or two?" I say.

"At least. Maybe three."

We wear masks when we walk into town.

When we pick up groceries, we don't go into the store. I call ahead and give them the list of what we need. We pay with a credit card over the phone. Then we wait outside in the car and someone from the store brings the bags out and loads them in the trunk of the car.

We know a woman who died of the virus. Sybil. A bright, talkative woman. She always dyed her hair magenta. I don't know how she got infected.

When we heard she was on a ventilator, we knew it was bad. People with COVID don't seem to recover once they're on a ventilator. And then they die and there is no funeral because the funeral homes are all closed up. Three weeks it took for her to die. I see her at moments in my mind, and I hear her voice and her laugh, and it makes me sad. Both of us. I tell Peter I might dye my hair magenta, and we both feel sad.

Then there was news on the radio that Terrence McNally and John Prine died of COVID. Peter plays John Prine albums on some evenings, by the open window in the living room with a book in his lap. The song "Sam Stone" makes him even sadder.

He's reading *Les Misérables,* he tells me. He's halfway through it and reads before he falls asleep at night. He says he has 642 pages left.

"I'm in no hurry. I don't feel the pressure I used to feel to finish books anymore," he says, "like before, when I'd rush to finish one so I could add it to my Goodreads list."

"We need mulch for the front garden," I tell him. "And a light bulb for over the sink."

"Okay," he says and writes those down on his list.

We do a lot of gardening now, planting bulbs and perennials, mostly. We walk on the beach in the late afternoons when the sun is still strong and the people are few, and the light burnishes our arms and faces. People wave from a distance if they recognize us with our masks on. We keep apart from everyone. I don't know what we'll do when it gets too cold to go out again.

I see my students remotely. I love to see them, and they hold their children up to the computer camera. The children tell me their names, and then they sit on their mothers' laps while we do algebra problems. After Peter has spent the morning mowing the lawn or painting one of the bedrooms or writing, he brings me coffee and a sandwich for lunch.

"I have come to realize," he tells me, "this is the way it's going to be for a long time. The house, the yard, ourselves, is all we have."

"I know, but I hope it won't last that long," I say. "I'm so afraid of getting sick and dying in pain, alone, without you to be with me. I want it to be over and for us to be safe."

"I'm afraid too," he tells me, "but isn't it good that we have each other, being together, with time to do the things we want? I think it's freeing. A kind of freedom I haven't felt since we were first married."

"What on earth do you mean, Peter? This is freedom? What kind of freedom is being confined to home? To this town? Marking the days like *X*s on a cell wall? It's getting old pretty quickly, don't you think? What's the point of doing all of the reading, exercising, weeding? To what end?"

"That's it," he says. "It's an end in itself. Doing what I love."

"Peter, we have children, grandchildren, who we don't see. Don't you want to see them? Museums? Restaurants? Protests? The park? You're giving up on that? There are bigger things, much more important things than painting a wall and replacing a light bulb. Black lives matter. Climate change. The stuff that makes a difference in the world."

"Yes, they do. They all matter. It's just that the past few months, here with you, have been good. Our time together. The quiet. In the end, it all comes down to how you spend the time you have."

"I'm not disagreeing," I tell him. "It's just, you always say to me that 'life is a journey, not a destination.' A journey takes you places, Peter. And now you're making a destination out of this place in this terrible time?"

"Can't it be? Just till there's a vaccine? Till the numbers go down?"

"And what if there is no vaccine? What if there's another virus? Then what?" I tell him, my voice raised in a way I don't like. "Yes, let's enjoy our time together, but don't imagine that reading and looking through old pictures and snipping daisies counts as a meaningful life. Not in the world we live in. Not in the world I want to live in. We can wear masks and assess our risks and make wise choices, and we can do that together. But believing in the good and working toward it is the journey I want. Flourishing, growing, learning, helping, making things better, bringing creativity into the world. I know you believe in all of that too."

"I do," he says, "but I feel like we're being buffeted by an unrelenting brutal storm, like the one the other night. All of us, this country, not just by the virus, but the anger, the politics."

We don't talk for the rest of the day.

In the morning, he comes in with the last of the rhubarb stalks in his hand. He leaves his shoes at the door.

"Steve Inskeep," I tell him, "said that Arizona has the highest per capita number of new cases in the world. Bahrain was fourth, and Nick Cordero died."

I can see by his face that I have said the wrong thing. I am caught between wanting to keep in touch with the world and not wanting to upset him with news.

He lays the rhubarb on the counter and leaves me alone. I don't like how I feel. I don't want to see the sadness in his eyes. I follow him into the bedroom and sit next to him on our bed.

"Peter, I have no problem with the way we are living now," I tell him. "We are doing what is necessary and prudent. I love the time we have together. I love the beach and the garden. The Zoom friends. The time to read and think. I love what we have learned we can live without, but also what I truly cherish and want to have restored. I'm adjusting to working from home, but it's not the same as seeing my students in person. I like going to a baseball game, working out in the gym with my friends, going to the city and having dinner in Wo Hop after a movie at the Angelica. I want all of that again."

He looks at me and sighs like he always does when he feels overwhelmed, even by the little things.

"You can't hide, Peter. You can't hide and say you like it. Engagement is the stuff of life. New ideas, creativity. The rest is stagnation, and I am not up for that. I don't want to take crazy risks, but I cannot close the doors and watch a constant series of reruns. Nor can you. We are imprisoned. There will always be home, a haven, a shelter from the storms, but it grows stale, and I need to open the windows and doors and get out."

"Staleness," he tells me, "is a small price. We're the fortunate ones. You know this. There are others, others who have no options and have to work in places that put them at great risk. There are many thousands suffering now, seeing people they love suffer and die. We have choices that most people don't have. The only thing we can do to help is for us to keep from getting infected."

And then he goes out into the yard, probably to give me some space, and I think, *I know he's right. It's the right thing to do. It's the unknown that is so unnerving to me. It's always been that way. I feel lost. Unmoored.*

And after a short time, he comes back in. "I know how you feel. I want all that too. I promise you, we'll get back to all we had as soon as we can."

His hands are dirty and stained with mulch. He reminds me that we bought the mulch we needed. I pick up my gardening gloves and go out with him, and soon we are up to our elbows mounding the roses in the front yard in readiness for the winter that is coming all too soon.

Traveling Light

Most able-bodied men of my father's generation—at least those lean white men who stayed out of trouble with the law and the union and who wanted to work—had work to do for as long as they wanted it, sometimes staying with the same company and moving up through the ranks, much as they had done in the army.

They each had two or three good, ironed white shirts, a couple of ties they were comfortable wearing, a few undershirts and shorts, two or three short-sleeved shirts, a decent pair of shoes, and one brown and one blue suit in the closet.

They didn't complain. They didn't talk much about things in general and never about what they did when they were away from home in the service or about what other folks, like their children, thought were the actually important stuff of life—like, for example, what they were thinking or feeling or why they never went to the doctor or wanted to go on vacation, or why they chose to keep all of that stuff corked up inside like a shaken bottle of Moxie that had been sitting too long in the sun.

And then they retired, still in what was considered at that time as reasonably good health, with a pension or social security or an investment of sorts from the company they had given the best years, hours, and days of their lives to, to live a few more years adjusting to imposed idleness and living in very close proximity with a woman who they assumed they loved but knew very little about. A woman they disagreed with on almost every issue, issues that had at least two sides and sometimes only one side, from the proper way to unroll toilet paper and close the toothpaste to how often is too often to visit with her mother in Manhattan on a Sunday afternoon when the lawn needed to be mown and the sun was shining.

They watched Martin and Lewis or Abbott and Costello on TV and laughed in the tight, self-conscious way they approached all joy.

They spent time alone. They ate what was put in front of them. They made things from the scrap that others had discarded. They never threw anything away. They had few things they cherished and fewer things they'd take with them to a desert island. They made do.

They took up some pastimes like golf or tennis or reading *Reader's Digest Condensed Books* and Tom Clancy novels or thinking about going fly-fishing.

On Father's Day, they were given golf balls and ceramic figurines of slump-shouldered, pot-bellied men in hats holding a fishing rod or a tennis racquet or some such evidence of their chosen recreation close by their side.

These figurines never got returned to the store. Each sat on the mantel or the desk in the spare bedroom or on the bookcase in the living room until one day it was placed on the table with a small lamp and a box of tissues and reading glasses next to a bed with aluminum railings and a handset that could be used to raise or lower the angle of the bed to make eating soft foods or sleeping easier. This was done in a pale, yellow-painted room that was shared with a frail, old Italian barber whose children came to visit on weekends in the winter, bringing wide-noodle and sausage casseroles and changes of bathrobes and bedclothes, children who brushed their father's hair as he sat in the soft-cushioned chair by the light through the window in the common room.

And the men waited for one of their children to visit and to bring their own children, who would stand by the bed and wait until they could walk beside the wheelchair and stop at the vending machine where Grandpa would hand them each the coins to insert and push the buttons for their choice of sweet.

And then, the figurine and the photographs of the grandchildren would be put gently into an empty shoe box and taken back to an equally empty home.

And once the kids agreed to sell the house on the quiet street, the figurine, perhaps by mistake, would be tossed into the green roll-off dumpster that had been backed into the driveway, along with the *Reader's Digest* books, the hat with the tea-colored sweat stains that never was washed, and the tennis shoes with dried red clay adhered to the treads and the hole in the toe. These things would be carted away, leaving deep gouges in the driveway that the man, if he were alive, would fill in with black asphalt patch while squinting and enduring the smell of the noxious petrochemicals. He would use a tamping tool made from a broom handle, duct tape, four two-inch number-eight slotted flat-head wood screws taken from a Mason jar he'd kept in the basement, and a spare piece of two-by-four that he had once painted red and used one summer as the runner in a four-wheeled two-seater go-cart he made for the kids before they got too big and wanted a '57 Chevy instead, then moved away to have children of their own.

Dear Malachi, Your Sister the Zen Is Moving to Alabama: A Conversation in Text

Malachi, how are you? I am at my wit's end. Your father says not to worry, I've been there before, and I always find that I have a little bit more string on that line. But this time I think he's wrong. It's your sister, Felicia. She told me she is moving to Alabama. I have nothing against Alabama, mind you, but Alabama? I mean, who goes from 72nd Street and 5th with a view of the park to Tuscaloosa? What does she know from Tuscaloosa? What kind of *mishigas* is that? I don't know what to do. I hear they don't wear masks there.

Ma, I'm okay. Of course they wear masks in Alabama. Don't believe everything you hear on the radio. Why is she going to Alabama?

I didn't hear that on the radio. And don't be so smart. Freida has a cousin whose son went to Alabama, Mobile, and he never came back.

What happened to him?

Nothing happened to him. He got a job. He's a big-shot lawyer. She says he makes good money and has a big house, nothing like you could get here for the money.

So?

So, he met a girl and got married, and Frieda says she never sees him, and she thinks he never goes to shul anymore. Your father says he's an atheist. How many atheists do you think are in Alabama? Four?

Ma, but why is Felicia going to Alabama? And I'm sure there's more than four. Who cares, anyway?

Felicia, my Jewish daughter, is going with her karate sensei, who I think she has a crush on, to what, become a Zen person like him? Your father says at least that's better than being an atheist. Or a socialist. I don't know what to do.

Ma, there is nothing to do. She's an adult. She's looking for herself. Her path. Whatever. Looking for the meaning of life.

What do you mean, the meaning of life? You think life has a meaning? Listen, to me, you get born, you die, and in the meantime, you make dinner.

That's funny, Ma.

I'm not being funny. If life had meaning, don't you think we'd all know about it? Someone would tell someone. Word would get around. Some things have meaning. Like algebra has meaning. Life doesn't. Everybody knows about algebra. We learn it in school. That's because algebra has meaning. You have x, and you have y, and you get z. Boom. That's the meaning of algebra. No big mystery. Your father says God tells us the meaning of life. Who said so? I tell him. My grandmother knew more about what's what than God. At least she knew a good man when she saw one and she knew how long it takes for bread to rise. And it didn't take her forty years wandering in the desert, walking in circles, eating matzoh to figure that one out. And don't tell me they ate manna. Where'd that come from? God? Why didn't he send them *kasha varnishkes* and pastrami along with some directions?

Ma, don't you really think that life has meaning? I mean love and things like that?

Malachi, I am sorry to say this to you, but in the words of Tina Turner, what's love got to do with it? You should read your history. Mesopotamia, Gilgamesh, Peloponnesia, Genghis Khan, Stalin, Hitler. Nixon, Pol Pot, Boko Haram. Mitch McConnell. How's all that for love? As you would say, give me break!

Ma, you sound so cynical. I'm surprised.

Malachi? Cynical? You live as long as I have, and things start to add up. This has not been a good year. Maybe you think it's unusual. It's not. What's unusual is that we have to wear masks and keep away from everyone. Big deal. First of all, is that so horrible? And second, you think we have it so bad? You tell me how good the Melians had it by the Athenians. Or the Canaanites and Amalekites, all massacred by the Israelites, or the Congolese, Sumerians, Armenians, Yemeni, Aztecs, Anasazi. The Rohingya. Shall I go on? Do we learn anything from the violence, foreign and domestic? No, we just shake our heads and keep walking. "Nothing to see here, folks. Move along." You think COVID is a plague? It's no plague. It didn't have to get like this. The plague is politics. Ego, money, drone strikes, napalm, and politics. That's the world's oldest plague.

I'm sorry.

Malachi, don't be sorry. Look, life's no party. Never has been. If life was such a big party, how come we didn't invite all the folks in Mumbai or Bangladesh, Nairobi or Karachi? You think all the fat cats in the world just forgot to let two billion people who live on a dollar and a quarter a day, if that much, know about all the big doings going on?

Ma...

Don't give me "Ma." I'm sorry, Malachi, I have to say it. I just don't think we all get it yet. Maybe we never will. The seas will rise, the crops will die, the forests will burn. You'd think we might just give a damn about someone else, give a person a hand, ease up on the gas a little, and say something nice. This year should've taught us that "all for me and the hell with you" doesn't work. You don't shit in the stream because you can. It all runs downhill, and that's where the corn grows.

Ma, I know you're right. I love you.

Malachi, I know you do. I love you too. I'm sad that Felicia is moving away. It's not the Zen thing. She's probably right, anyway, hitting exit, reset, with all that's going on. Maybe it's good for her as long as a crocodile doesn't eat her. I miss her already.

Alligators. Alligators live in Alabama, not crocodiles.

Okay. If an alligator doesn't eat her. What a horrible thought, anyway. I hate this texting thing. Call me later.

The Woman in a Purple Velvet Coat at the Edge of the Surging Sea

On the eve of my sixtieth birthday, I dreamed I was a woman in a hooded purple velvet coat.

She (Me), standing on the jagged, angular geometric rocks at the edge of the surging, curling sea.

It was evening, and the wind blew hard as it does when the moon is full and high, and the heat of the day fades, and the ozone-lavender lithium light rises off the water and becomes the sky.

It was in the crepuscular hour. The time between the exhaustion of the waking day and the wonders of the unknown night. The hour when you could imagine yourself to be of one mind and also of another, in unison. In a settled, common unison. When yes and no are equal to the task of living and breathing and waking and sleeping and lifting and falling.

And the wind blew from the east, and the wind blew from the west. And yet my coat was unruffled. It hung down from my shoulders to the toes of my shoes.

My black shoes reflected the moonlight. The shoes I danced in as a girl. The shoes that I wore at my baptism in the faith and on the first day of school and on the day my mother died.

The shoes my father taught me to lace. The shoes so soft and snug and sturdy they filled my body with strength and soulfulness.

I held the moon in my hand, and the waves curled under it. The waves of blue and white. The waves I felt I could walk away on. Walk to the moon on.

I was a girl-woman. I was a woman-girl. I was my mother's child. My child's mother. The slow admixture of young and old. Of constancy and change in the moment. Of the years I had lived and the years I have not yet lived. The years before I was birthed and the years beyond the end.

My mother had worn a purple coat. The color of sadness and mourning set against the midnight black of her hair.

I stood at the edge of the sea. In the crepuscular light. In the coat my mother wore. In the coat my child will wear. In the moonlight in which my mother bathed and at which she wondered. The light that reveals and shadows, both. The softest light. The silent light.

I stood, a woman-mother-child, at the edge of the surging, curling sea in the lavender air and entrusted myself to the mysteries I did not know, could not know, and the wonders I knew I would never know.

And I stood with all of that. In the edge of the day and the night, and the dark and the light, and the light and the dark, in my hooded purple velvet coat that my mother had once worn before me.

Reading the Book of Exodus by Candlelight

Sally Robinson turned away from the kitchen window. The first purple crocuses were pushing up through the last patches of crusted backyard snow.

It always started with the crocuses.

Jesus Christ! she thought. "The damn crocuses," she said.

Henry, her husband of eleven years, heard her and said nothing. He knew what was coming.

A wave of dread seeped up like marsh gas from the pit of her stomach. Henry saw it in her face, that underwater look. His heart sank.

She hated Passover. Like her mother hated Easter. The preparation. The work. The house cleaning. The changes of the dishes. The food to be thrown out. The food she must prepare.

She was a smart woman. Patient, rational, and reasonable. She was Jewish, but not *that* Jewish. She had converted. She knew the story. Slavery. Oppression. The persecution. The killing. "I get it," she would say. But in the end, she hated it in a way she could neither articulate nor explain.

Henry, though, now felt that it was the right thing to do. His parents were not observant. They didn't keep kosher. But his father had been in the war. He had fought the Germans. Not in the actual fighting. But he would have if they had sent him over.

The war had changed Henry. He'd seen the skeletal photographs of the Jews. The piles of bones. Everyone had. The evil men could do and could abide. He needed a way to bear witness. He, too, found it hard to find the words for it all, but observing the Passover seemed a foothold. A way to honor his father.

For ten years. More. It had been the same. Sally had her questions and complaints. And for each one, Henry had provided an answer.

"Please, Henry, just this one year can we simply wash the regular dishes in the dishwasher? The sterilize cycle. Twice?" she pleaded.

"Sally," he said, "that is not what we were commanded to do. Do you think they had a dishwasher in Egypt?"

"No, do you think they had two sets of dishes? Four, if you count the *milchidik* and *fleyshik* sets. Did they have Streit's matzohs in three flavors and Easter colors?"

"Of course not. But we do. And we do this now because they couldn't. And because those who did it were killed for only that one reason."

"But, Henry, I don't believe. You don't, either. This is your own crusade, not mine."

"I am not asking you to believe. All I ask is that you do this for me because I love you."

"I know you do. But does that mean I have to turn this house upside down for two weeks? To show that we know that people have suffered? Been murdered? Been enslaved? Spent forty years in the wilderness eating goats every night and manna every morning and drinking magic water? Where did that come from, anyway? And for what? So that we can eat *cholent* and drink Manishewitz, leaning on a pillow? There are other better ways...better ways to remember and to make a difference."

"We need to honor the suffering."

"What? By making me suffer? I already know what that's like."

"Stop," he said. "You're sounding like your mother."

"No, you stop. Don't tell me about my mother. That's your answer for everything. This is not about my mother. It's about me.

Listen to me! I don't want to do this. Not now. Not anymore. Why can't you just hear that?"

Each year, she gathered up the chametz, all the leavened food and whatever it might have touched. Cleaned the refrigerator, the freezer, the drawers, each room, each closet, the basement, the car. Dealt with the doughnut crumbs, the dog's food, and the cosmetics, burning it all in the trash can on the porch.

And every year she stood at the bottom of the attic steps and Henry handed down the cartons of green glass dishes with the fluted edges. And she soaked them clean and filled the cupboards she had scrubbed and lined with flowered shelf paper.

She shopped, chopped, made horseradish, roasted the egg and the chicken neck and the brisket, the burnt offering. *A burnt offering? Are you kidding?*

"Don't walk away," she said, because that was what he had started to do. "Stay with me. Here. Talk to me."

He turned back to face her. "Can we do it just one more year, and then no more?"

"No."

"Why no?"

"Because that way is meaningless," she told him.

"How can you say that?"

"Henry. You mean well, but you read from the Haggadah words you don't understand while your father falls asleep and the dinner gets cold and your nieces fight over the afikomen for the dollar you will give them. And the next day, we are no different from the day before. The symbols have become some self-congratulating abstraction. Do they ever make us feel better or change the state of the world?"

Her brown eyes were resolute. She had never talked to him like this before. He stood with his arms at his sides.

"Pick one thing," she said. "One thing that you can truly say means the most to you about Passover and I will pick one thing. But don't pick the wine because that is what I want to pick. And that will be our Passover."

"Can I pick two?"

"Okay," she said.

And on the first night of Passover, while his relatives gathered at Aunt Ethel's in Flatbush and hers went over to cousin Elaine's on the island, Sally and Henry sat in their dark kitchen in the glow of two lit candles and ate matzohs that Sally had baked from scratch and drank the wine that Henry had bought at the shop in town by the train station. They scooped up the warm charoses they had made together.

And for the next seven days, in the evening, by the candle-light, they read the entire book of Exodus, a little bit each night, reading each and every line and every single one of the footnotes, and talked very, very late into the night.

SOMEBODY TO LOVE

Our first long training run was along Ocean Parkway. A flat, straight road running east from Jones Beach toward Gilgo and Captree. The beach was on our right, hidden behind high, grassy, midday dunes.

Larry set the pace. Hard and fast. Like a driving tom-tom: eighth notes in 4/4 time. The two of us.

I was Jack Bruce on bass to his Ginger Baker on drums. Keith Richards to his Charlie Watts. Like Jack Casady to his Spencer Dryden running the bass line on "Somebody to Love."

The parking lot at the Oak Beach Inn was packed full. All the beach lots were. Cars waiting for spots to open were held in check by park rangers. Lines of cars were stopped between the beach entrances.

Girls stood beside pink-painted VWs or leaned back, elbows bent, against wide, black Ford F-150 tailgates, legs crossed in cutoff jeans. White pocket flaps peeked out below the fingerlike fringes high up at the top of their Bambi-colored thighs. They waved Coronas. Smiled like peaches in the sun. Radios set to BLS.

Larry looked at them without breaking stride. He always looked at the women. He loved looking at the women. His eyes were drawn to them like a wedding reception guest's eyes are drawn to the standing rib roast.

Doing eight-minute miles, we did the first twenty in a little over two and a half. If we kept up, we'd do the 26.2 to Captree in three-forty-nine.

He's screwing a woman at work.

No doubt she's told him her husband doesn't understand her. He's probably said the same thing to her about Meredith. He probably told her he loves her. He probably thinks that it's true.

He's never said a word about it to me. We never talk about that kind of thing. I know, though, for a fact, that his wife *does* understand him. She *totally* and *completely* understands him. Without any doubt, she understands him fifty times better than he understands himself. She's the one who told me.

"He's thirty-nine," she said, "and he has a dick. What else do you expect? He can't get over the fact that in '69 he had a kid, an 8.5% mortgage, and a bald spot. The river of free love, drugs, and rock and roll was flowing swiftly past him, and that river flowed in only one direction. The only really free love he could have had then was the only one he didn't want," she told me.

We hit Captree in just under four. Took off our shoes and walked down to the water. He pulled off his shirt.

"Great run," I said. He nodded.

The water was clear and green. The waves were high and loud. He grabbed my arm and pulled me toward the water. We dove through the waves.

When we came out, I turned away from him, out toward the water.

I love running with him. He paces me. Pushes me. Past what I ever thought I could do. Running beside him, step for step, breathing easily, it feels like I could run forever.

"Let's get a drink," I said, my back to him, peeling away my soaked, clinging shirt from my body. When I turned back toward him, he was looking at me.

At my tits.

"Okay, tiger, enough!" I said.

"I wasn't looking. Besides, there isn't that much to see," he said in that thickened, fourteen-year-old, gonadal, hard-on-induced voice he gets as if his salivary glands, in sympathy with his testicles, have swollen his airway half closed.

"You were too," I said. "You had that Daytona Beach spring break weekend look on your face."

"It was only a quick glance."

"It wasn't *quick* and it wasn't a *glance*. It was a full, two-handed, lingering eye-grope. You thought I couldn't see you looking."

I leaned over the water fountain. He was a little behind me. I could see him rearranging himself in his running shorts. I thought about what it would be like if I turned around while he was doing it. "Just a quick glance, Tarzan," I'd say. But I didn't.

His wife knows all about him. "The new one," she said, "teaches English. She graduated two years ago from Barnard. You'd think she'd know better. God knows, he doesn't. She has a flat stomach, a tight ass, and legs like steel."

"How do you know that?" I asked her.

"How do I know that? He's never uttered the word *Barnard* before in his life. And now he's said it two dozen times in the last month. I'm there slicing eggplant and he's like, 'Hey, you think we could afford to send Lydia to Barnard when she's ready for college?' Or 'Didn't Chuck's sister go to Barnard?' I'm not saying he's an idiot, but he could play a convincing one on TV. Lydia is four and a half."

"No. I mean the 'legs like steel' thing," I recall saying.

"The woman who works in the principal's office at the high school where he works knows my friend Eileen, and she plays mahjong with us when one of us can't make it. And so, she filled in for me the week I had my wisdom tooth out and she told Eileen she sees them sneak out for 45-minute lunch breaks together, and she swore Eileen to total secrecy. That's how I know."

We'd parked my car in the Captree lot and drove back to the lot at Jones Beach, Field One, where his car was.

In the car, we talked about running New York in the fall together.

"New York has hills, big ones," he said. "It's not like this. Don't expect to finish in sub-four."

"We should start running hills," I said. "Maybe in two weeks. Molly is away that weekend. We could run out to Sag Harbor."

He never asks me about Molly. We've been together for almost as long as he's been with Meredith. We sometimes have dinner with him and Meredith. Molly and I make like we don't know what's going on with them. He acts like Molly is my roommate. Even when she twirls her fettucine alfredo around the tines of her fork and guides it into my mouth, her palm just below my chin.

I know he's a dick. With his desperately permed hair he thinks covers his bald spot. I don't have to like him. I just love running with him.

IN THE WAVES OF WAKING

In the waves of waking this morning, I was troubled by a thought I had about the earth. Not the melting and heating of it or the heaving upwards or the sinking of it beneath the sea or the mudslides and fires and the dust clouds of it now—things I worry and think about, and read and talk about, to the degree of obsession—but this morning, just the turning of it.

The turning of it. The simple rotation of it.

In the waves of my own sinking and rising through the layers of sleep, the question of which way the earth turns became weighted and unsettling. Because I found, in my half-sleep, that I could not answer it. *This is something I should know. Something we all surely know.*

Is it from the east to the west or from the west to the east? The simple answer was simply elusive to me. More than elusive: troubling in its inaccessibility. More than troubling: a gripping doubting of my own mental capacity, my ability to retrieve what is known. What I once surely had known.

My daughter is flying tomorrow from Boston to LA. East to west. Her first flight alone. The alone part worries her. I feared flying when I was younger. Crashing. Dying. I was frozen by the thought of it. My mother gave me one of her Valium pills. It helped. But upon landing in San Juan, in my Bermudas and sandals, I realized that I would need to remain there. I feared the return trip. I had not planned for the return flight—for the extra pill I would need. The return trip, the thinking of it, the worry about it, even

83

being on the beach—Luquillo Beach—it stole the present from me. Stole the softness of the sand, the warmth of the sun, the breeze in my hair. *How the uncertain future can so easily steal the present.* The fear of the unknowable future robbing the reality of the present.

But…to the turning of the earth. Like a clock. Or not like a clock. And if like a clock, from what perspective?

The sun in the sky. Its rising and setting. The orange-scarlet sky in the mornings and the pink and purple in the evenings. Rising over the water here and setting over the land.

This simple point—the direction of the turning—is something I should know. The turning that creates our days and nights. The transit of the Milky Way. The days by which we measure the hours that fill the years of our lives.

I know that I know this. Long have known this. As I know left from right and up from down. Tall and short. Past and present. As I know who I am and the names of my children.

There are things I don't expect to remember. Like the name of the actor, the tall one whose wife died, I think, in a ski accident, like Sonny Bono did. Hitting her head into a stanchion, I think. But the actor. The tall one with hair that likes to flop across his forehead. Endearing him. Softening him. And his voice, also soft. The heartfelt seriousness of it. *It will come to me.* And the singer. The drummer of a band. British. The band was named for him, or maybe not. I see them both in my mind. Their names elude me. They will come to me, too, if I don't think of them. Later, when I'm making toast or washing the dishes. *Liam Neeson.*

It doesn't worry me much when the names don't come. It's not as though they ever were so much a part of what I knew, needed to know, that I could not step around the emptiness of the erasure and go on with what I was doing. I easily made do without the name. *Phil Collins.* But the name of my son. That name comes instantly to me with ease, as does my own name. But I think about the day I will not know his name. Or perhaps my own.

The day I will know it but not be able to find these among the other things I had securely settled in my brain. To use them. More important than the house keys or my glasses.

As I woke, I thought that remembering the way the earth turns and causes the winds to blow and in which time seems to move would never be difficult. I'd always be able say with confidence, "Sure, I know that. How could I not know that?"

I went into the kitchen to make the coffee and I stood by the window and saw the sun in sky, and I knew from where it had risen, its arc, and where it would set later.

And I drew a rough picture of the earth and the sun on a scrap of paper and arrows to plot out the spin in my mind. To reason it out. The logic of it. The science of it.

The penciled lines were momentarily reassuring. But I know that I may not always know how to do that. That not only would the answer be irretrievable, but I may lose the ability to restore it. And with that, loosening my assured grip on reality.

I worry about that. It is an essential, almost constant worry. It is the way that the future is stealing my present. Starting with an easily dismissed sense out-of-sync-ness but progressing to an unsettling knowledge of out-of-touch-ness.

Perhaps, if that theft happens, I won't take notice of it…and let it be as it is when all time is present time.

The Bright and Shining Cities on the Hill

Hobbes paid good money for the boat. One hundred euros. He bought the outrigger from a young native of the island. A man named Paolu. The boat was serviceable and easily repaired. Paolu threw in the few simple tools he might need. For free.

He bought a sail, too, and two weighted twine nets from another man. An older man. A muscled and bent fisher with a strong black back.

Paolu was moving his family to Fiji with other families from the island. A ship was expected at the end of the month. This would be the last one before the start of the cyclone season.

The island was one of the most astonishingly beautiful places Hobbes had ever seen.

"Do you have sons and daughters?" Paolu wanted to know.

"I do."

"Why are they not here with you?"

"This is not a place for them. They have their own families and jobs to do. They live in cities. They have lives of their own."

"I think," Paolu said, "they would like to be with you."

"You may be right, but I have lived alone for a long time. It's the way I am most comfortable."

Hobbes moved his things into a house on the north end of the island, near the highest point of land where it was rocky, flat, and dry. Where he could wake each morning to the sun rising over the fine curve of the sea. Where he could watch the storm clouds billow and rise, turning gray underneath. From where the cyclones approached, and the seas surged.

The house had survived the cyclone in 2015. Then the one in 2020.

He brought along his books. A radio. A two-band shortwave Kaito KA-500 solar and hand-crank he had bought on eBay. A desalination unit. A knife and flints. A thin, oiled canvas tarp.

He planned to stay in the house on the island. Eat taro and fish as long as he was able. Read Steinbeck, Nietzsche, and Saramago. Teach himself French and Maori. And he would stay after the others left—the young ones with families and the old ones who would be the last to go when, finally, they owed more to the past than to the present.

He would stay past when the seawater infiltrated the wells and flooded the soil and covered the landing strip the Americans built in the war and the copra exporters used. Past when the winds bent and blew down the last of the coconut palms. Past when the sea rose to push against the steepest of the slopes. Past the time when Fiji had sent the last of its ships. He would stay even then.

A young man who lived in Sheffield, a reporter from *The Guardian,* came to speak with him. He had already spoken to Hobbes's daughter.

His daughter told him she would never speak to Hobbes again if he did this. She could not abide this, she'd told him. Would never forgive him. It was his daughter who had called *The Guardian.*

The reporter from Sheffield asked him if he thought that, in the end, anyone would care one whit about what he was doing. He asked Hobbes if he was dying of some terminal disease.

"No," he said.

Did he think that Shell Oil or Amazon or OPEC would give a damn?

He said he didn't know.

"When did you make this decision?" the reporter wondered. "What was the turning point for you?"

Hobbes told him that it was when he learned that Disney and other megacorporations were building entire cities, not just bunkers, but completely self-contained cities—Ararat, they called them—high in the mountains. The Chattahoochees near DC, and one in the Green Mountains with light-rail service from Boston and New York, and another in the Sierra Nevada and in the San Bernardinos. And yet another one in the Blue Ridges.

"I thought about these shining, protected cities on the hills," he said, "for the oil and investment bankers and the Silicon-Valley rich. Building these redoubts from the coming horror while Jakarta, Houston, New Orleans, Dhaka, London, and Mumbai will all be left to sink below the surface when their shoddy, pregnable, and useless seawalls and levees are breached, and all who live there with nowhere else to go will surely die."

He continued, "When it became unavoidably clear to me that those very same people willingly and knowingly allowed and perpetrated the coming disaster for their own gain. That they ignored the dire warnings of the continued burning of fossil fuels and dragged, if not dug in, their heels and did nothing to stop it. As if the poorest and most powerless of the earth's people were worth nothing, like wretched nobodies. I knew that all hope I had for a just world was lost. That the rich will survive and thrive, and the rest of world, the other world that fed and served them, and washed their dishes and made their clothes, and sheltered them, and cleaned their toilets, will simply and forever disappear."

"And you know what will happen to you too, don't you?"

"Yes," Hobbes told him. "I do."

"And you still will let the ships leave without you?"

"Yes, this is the only thing I can do. The only thing that has meaning to me anymore. I can no longer bear witness and not act.

But you, you can be my witness. And when the waters cover Tuvalu and Samoa and Fiji and the Maldives, and all the rest of the islands, you will know that I am gone too, and while it will likely strike many as a foolish man's choice, it may also be a call for a moral action on the part of those who can make a real difference."

Waiting in Line at the Church of the Transfiguration

Moriah held a place in line for Max. The sidewalk in front of the church was dry and gray, and the late December wind banked around the corner from Fifth Avenue and west along East 29th Street. It was all she could do to keep her balance against the wind, what with one hand atop her head to keep her fur Bergman-like pillbox firmly in place and the other holding her gray overcoat gripped tight around her and securing the nosegay of three red tea roses and some frilled greens close to her chest.

The hat cost more than she could afford. The nosegay was unnecessary, but her mother had paid for it. Reluctantly.

Moriah touched her chin. She had covered a small, raised pimple with cosmetic her mother had given her. Nerves, her mother had said. She looked at the other couples in the queue. The way they were dressed. What shoes they wore.

She politely excused herself, changing her place in line twice, three times, moving to the end of the line to let other couples, arms entwined, move up in the line ahead of her, thankful, apologetic looks on their faces.

Max had come with her. But he had left the license on the dresser in his bedroom at his parents' apartment on Broadway and had to take two buses uptown, to retrieve it, and back to meet her before the rector closed the doors at noon.

Her mother, if she knew what was happening, would say, "Don't hold your breath waiting for him, Moriah. But no worries—if he doesn't show, I can return the flowers to Adler's if they still have some signs of life in them."

There was a rush to marry.

The war had started it. Pearl Harbor. The Nazis. The Italians. The Japanese. Roosevelt had made it imperative, not so much the rush to marry but the sense of existential threat. Everyone felt it.

The country was attacked, and that demanded an immediate response. The need to martial resources, to rally to fight, to sacrifice, to do what the country needed of you. Get your hands dirty. Offer up your life for it if that's what it took.

Urgency grew up from the soil, filled the air with its pungency, flowed in the insistent streams of voices—the radio broadcasts, the news hawkers on the streets, the neighbors in the lobbies of apartments and office buildings. It was unavoidable and insatiable.

Moriah felt the threat to the well-ordered life she'd imagined, and she'd invested in. Planned on. Hoped for. A marriage. A wedding. A home. Children. A happy life. All of it was threatened by a world she had no control over. If she could get a job, she would. What would she do, though? Steno? War work of some sort. Not at all what she had planned on.

There was all that and then there was Max. Brown hair and soft brown eyes. An off-center smile.

They'd danced. Fast and slow. In the rushed rhythm of the moment. In small clubs, and at living room parties.

Max had signed up. To fight. To do what he was expected to do. He had asked her to wait for him, though he had no idea what waiting actually meant. How that feeling would translate into something real in his life. It, in fact, had no translation that entered his mind beyond the heroism of it. Of the sound of the words he said to her: "I have to go. Will you wait for me?" Words that seemed to flow out of him without thought. Without anything but the desire to go, to fight, to have meaning in life, to earn it, whatever *it* was. And to be wanted, admired, needed, waited for.

Of course she would wait for him. Though she, too, had no idea of what that meant, waiting for him. Of course she would wait until he came back. They'd marry. She would write him letters he would open in his barracks or in a trench somewhere with gunfire and aircraft overhead and thunder in the distance. There was sacrificial magic in it all.

They both felt the magic. Life had become magical. You would do what you were called to do. It was your duty.

And for both of them, the magic erased the unknown. The war became the known. And the known was the urgency of it.

"Marry me," she'd said.

So she stood in front of the church with her hair up like Olivia de Havilland. A dark blue suit. The small bouquet her mother had given her. There had been no time to plan for more than that.

In January, he rode the bus to Fort Worth. A green footlocker, half full.

Moriah lived with her mother until a month or two before the baby was due and planned to take the train to be with him, to have the baby there, in Texas. And they would be happy.

And all would be well. She would keep the house and care for the baby. He would see her when he could until his orders came. And then she would wait again for him.

And she did. She made the meals, cleaned the spills, washed the diapers and the dishes and the floors, and called the landlord when the sink or the toilet backed up. She endured the heat and the Texas humidity, paid the bills, called the doctor, and held the baby, the crying baby, the baby boy she had named for her father. There was always something baking in the oven or bubbling over on the stove or washing in the machine in the hall. She read popular novels. All were a measure of happiness because she was waiting.

And in August, in her housecoat with her hair undone, when she had not seen Max in a month, she was not happy. "When we move to San Diego, it will be better," she told her mother.

"Don't hold your breath."

And then it was to San Antonio, and Eagle Pass, and Brownsville.

And on a hot December afternoon on their tenth anniversary when the boy was nine and the girl was seven, Moriah waited in the still air and shade of the front porch for the delivery of the dryer they'd bought.

She'd have to tell the delivery man she couldn't accept it. They were moving again. She didn't know where.

She called her mother and told her that Max had gotten new orders. Korea. And asked if she could come back to New York and stay with her and wait until he came back.

"Of course, dear," her mother said. "Of course."

Hobbes's Good Intentions

Hobbes had come to stay on the island. To live and, more to the point, to live until he died. The island itself was dying. And again, more pointedly, the island was being killed. Inundated. Drowned.

Drowned by the sea. The Pacific. The same Pacific that had brought the fish and coral reefs, the warm winds, and the rainwater. The coconut palms, the breadfruit, the mangroves, the bananas, and the taro.

Hobbes had come to the island when the tipping point had been reached. When the Doomsday Clock had run past sixty-odd seconds before midnight. After the world had been warned and the climate commissions had made their predictions, after the treaties had been signed, the money had been promised, the deadlines had been missed, the wars had been fought, the children had died of starvation, the people had fled their homelands, and many had been left to die in refugee camps or in life rafts.

Hobbes had come to the island when the world's will to change never equaled the need for change.

He had come when there was still talk of the slight sliver of hope that the global warming past two degrees centigrade could still be stopped. That Bill Gates would stop it. Or the UN. Or someone, somehow. A sliver of hope, no matter how small, that was still seen as large enough to be used as an excuse to not actually act.

It was Hobbes's hope that when he came to the island, when he had declared that he would remain there until the waters rose so high that he would be swept away to die, he would capture the world's attention like a priest immolating himself on a street before an astonished crowd and cameras flashing, and that change would then come.

The people of the island stayed for a while and then they left in boats and planes to go to Fiji or other islands that would still take them. Hobbes remained as he said he would.

Then, one day, a large motorboat came to the island.

Hobbes was surprised at his ambivalence at seeing the boat approach and the three men who got off. One was the last islander to leave, another was the one who had sold him the house and the outrigger. The third was a very old man.

The old man called Hobbes by name. He carried a message from the islanders who had left. It was that Hobbes could no longer stay on the island.

"Mr. Hobbes," he said, "I thank you for wanting to bring attention of the world to our plight. However, now it is time for you to leave."

Hobbes looked at the old man. Put his rough hand to his forehead, rubbed it across his eyes. "But why?" he asked.

"Because," said the old man, "this is our island. Our people have lived here for thousands of years, and our ancestors' spirits will always live here. If you stay, you will only appropriate our voice, usurp our worth in the eyes of the world."

He continued, "The sea, when it took away our home, our food, our livelihood, our history, was not sufficient to bring the changes that were needed. You came in good faith, but if you stay and die here, you will be seen as the martyr. You will be the Christ on the cross. Your suffering and dying will be seen as more valuable, more horrific, than ours has been. Your sacrifice will count for more than ours.

"Mr. Hobbes," he said, "please go home. Go back to your family. Give your interviews to *The Guardian* in your comfortable living room and leave this place to us."

"Leave what place? There will be nothing left of this place for anyone."

"It is our home. It will always be our home. And when the seas recede, as they will, one day long after you have died and I have died and our children's children have died, our people will return to this island. It is our island, not Gilbert's Island or Hobbes's Island.

"Not the island of the man who once came to this place like a white savior when we, the native people of this island, carefully considered our options and, as a people in charge of our own destiny and with dignity, chose to leave it voluntarily, to leave it as it was when the sea had come to reclaim it for a while and to which we will certainly return one day.

"Not the island of the white extractors who came time and time again, taking minerals from our mountains and leaving behind slag heaps, polluting our valleys, building roads and runways over our land, selling us plastic spoons and T-shirts we have no use for, and bringing their schools and guns and firing ranges and atomic bombs.

"We are not ignorant. We did not bring upon ourselves the rising water and the storms, the acid that eats away the reef and kills the water plants and drives away the fish, and the heat and drought that empties our wells of fresh water.

"It is not we who are ignorant. It is you and your brothers who have ignored what the earth has been telling you year after year. It is they who are destroying our home and are responsible for the lives that have been lost through ignorance. Billions of animals, plants, fish, seabirds, insects, and whole habitats have been destroyed by the arrogance of their ignorance, never ever to exist again. And do they mourn them? Do they cry for them? Does this make them resolve to stop the murder? It does not.

"All their words and promises are meaningless. They have been of no help. Their deeds and their religion of the bulls and bears they worship above all else have brought this upon us. The marketplace where they buy and sell lives, where they place their faith and devotion that motivates their every thought, their every action, and blinds them to all else."

"I have given up all I have," Hobbes said. "I came here in the hope that people would respond and help. I am not like those others."

"I believe you are not," said the old man. "We mean no harm. We want the same as you do. But for now, we want to honor what is left to us."

At that, Paolu, the man whose boat Hobbes purchased, stepped forward and offered Hobbes an envelope with payment for the house, the nets, and the outrigger.

"I can't accept this," said Hobbes.

"Please do," said Paolu. "We have accepted our fate, Mr. Hobbes, and you can do no more for us. If you want to help the earth, go to where the resisters and deniers live. Build your hut along the Thames or Battery Park or Melbourne. We did not ask for you to come here, but now we ask for you to leave with us now and go speak to the power where the power lives. It is not here."

Hobbes did not agree with their reasoning. The poorest and least powerful people lived where it was the hottest. That is where the greatest harm was felt. The rich and powerful lived where it was cooler. They would not be swayed by his insignificant protest on the Thames or anywhere else like that. But he could not argue with the beliefs and the decisions of the islanders, and the only measure of autonomy left to them.

"Wait. I will get my things," he said.

Seize the Day

During a protracted period of convalescence following a rather routine surgery that resulted in a quite unfortunate, unpredictable and unexpected series of complications, more serious by far than the condition for which the surgery had been performed, I fell into a time of deep despair for which I could assign no reasonable cause and out of which I saw no apparent avenue of egress, though, I must admit, due only to an ill-considered intransigence on my part, I sought neither professionally qualified help nor the possible mitigation that might have been afforded by the use of widely available and efficacious prescription medications, or the less-costly advice of friends and the array of psychoactive formulations from which they routinely found relief from their own feelings of despair or disquietude, nor, as a last resort, the advice of my parents, who were still alive and in full control of their faculties, though with whom I had little contact and with whom I had a strained and awkward relationship, most especially with my father, who, as circumstance would have it, if I remember correctly, resolutely, for only the reason that he distrusted doctors and others in society who professed to have knowledge or skills he lacked, refused to have the same surgery I had undergone, despite having sustained a similar injury during a weekend game of doubles with three men of his approximate age and social status, all being solidly hardworking men living then in the relative comfort of a new suburban development, hastily created outside of the bustling city in which they had been raised and for which they had deep affection and allegiance, and from which they left, with little reluctance but great insistence from their wives as their financial circumstances improved, resulting, in no small degree, from the relative economic prosperity that arose in the postwar period and spread as tantalizingly as might the aroma of a cooling apple pie left on an open windowsill, during the rise of the Eisenhower middle class, and in a time when that sort of outward population diffusion, fueled by the rapid expansion of the network of interstate highways and interchanges, as well as the general perception among some groups that that was what was being done and what seemed to be expected of modern young families, what with wives who did not work out of the home and children who, according to the advice of well-respected clinical experts of the likes of Dr. Spock and others, were being encouraged to spend their time at home playing out-of-doors being free, even though, contrarily, in their own minds, that is, in the minds of the men themselves, the time they had spent playing stickball, skelly, or handball in the city streets dodging sedans or riding subway cars far afield from their own neighborhoods seeking fortune and adventure was the freest and best time of their lives and from which the memories that most sustained them in times of their own malaise and self-doubt were made, and which bore little or no resemblance to the fey, childish pursuits of their own children, which again, in the minds of the men themselves, were of little benefit and provided little of the toughening of body and spirit that the men felt was the object of the short time spent in youth and that would undoubtedly lead to a generation of coddled, complaining, namby-pamby, soft-skinned man-children in ill-fitting and unsubstantial suits, tight underwear, and thin-soled shoes from foreign countries, who would be wholly and woefully ill-prepared for the challenges that life would set before them and from which they would learn nothing, and that would send them crying back to their mothers for succor and protection, from whom they would undoubtedly receive the unflagging confirmation of the belief that the world, in fact, neither understood nor fully appreciated them and from which they should be parentally shielded, rather than forcibly separated from the unquestioning, commodious, and all-too-welcoming maternal bosom, and from whom, it was inevitable, the relief sought by the still-wet-behind-the-ear men-children could not be obtained because it was from these very same eternally capacious bosoms from which they had been weaned so incompletely, so belatedly, and so well beyond the time at which a clean break could have afforded both mother and child the distancing needed for the mental health of both of them, which would prepare them both for the harsh but inevitable exigencies of life in an exotic but unforgiving world full of both wonder and woe, opportunity and opposition, and, to be sure, the inescapable reality of decline and death, regardless of the good intentions of one's heart or the resolution of their beliefs and the contribution, evil or beneficent, they had made in their lives to the commonweal, and so, casting aside any hope of receptivity from my father, I sought to find some refuge and relief in a perusal of the books I had accumulated on my shelves over the years in the times I was flush with some expendable cash and relying upon the recommendations of the *New York Times Book Review* as well as books I had seen being read by strangers on trains, selecting particularly those books that the engrossed reader had been more than halfway through and that had that ineffable quality associated with the dimensions of the book as well as the thickness of the pages and the presence or absence of the deckling of the edges, more often favoring the deckled edge for reasons I cannot well explain and oftentimes finding an attraction in the way that the book might lay in the hand with the spine firmly held in the center and pages falling softly left and right over the palm as might a book of psalms or a Bible in the hands of a Southern Baptist preacher as he commands the hearts of the faithful, holding the book aloft as if it were a loosely swaddled babe in his hands with the strength of both his fingers and of his convictions and which he then cradles, the pages against his chest, as his voice rises and falls in gentle cadences, his point having been made, and I, hoping to find such a book, running my fingers across the shelved spines and sensing what I could by mere contact with what lay within the bound pages, as if the community of words contained within were communicated to me by an ineluctable and welcome force, that it came to be, through no volitional act on my part, that my fingers came to rest upon a used copy of Bellow's *Seize the Day,* which I recall purchasing on an afternoon in a long-ago September at the Brattle Book Shop in Boston, and which I had never read, as I was neither familiar with Bellow nor his writing, and it was within the pages of this book that I sought, with great hope and confidence in the title, to find the solace I so sorely desired and which, to my dismay I found, sadly, was not forthcoming, or more likely, the point of which I had missed, but be that as it may, I set the book aside and did what I should have done in the first place and called my mother in the hope that she could care for me as she had done, long ago, when I was young and feeling unwell.

Even the Dead Come Back to Remind Us

It was hot. Baking hot. The sun was slowly walking toward the deep end of July. July twenty-first. And Simon Zeckendorf was on the train going to work. Changing to the C at West 4th, he squeezed into the last empty seat in the car. The riders on either side were damp and overheated.

He couldn't concentrate. Opened and closed the book in his hand. *Swann's Way*. Proust. Wrapped in brown paper, as he'd felt it would seem pretentious to be seen standing in the subway holding a worn copy of Proust. He would surely think that if he'd seen someone else doing it.

Proust is hard going. He'd started reading it several times before, only to nod off a few pages in and set it aside for another time. Maybe he just wasn't up to the task. Maybe a new copy, a new translation, might give him a fresh start.

An article he'd read touted the brilliance of Proust, whose 149th birthday had just passed on July 10. One line he'd read wouldn't leave him alone. "Even the dead," it said, paraphrasing Proust, "when we least expect it, come back to remind us of their love and of our guilt."

Even the dead come back to remind us.

Death. Love. Guilt.

July birthdays. Births and deaths.

His mother's and his oldest daughter's birthdays came in July. One on the twenty-first and the other on the twenty-second. His mother, coincidentally, had died some years ago, also in July.

On his run the day before, through Sunset Park around the Green-Wood cemetery, he had tried to remember whose birthday was on which day, but he gave up. His wife, Bernadette, would know, he thought.

He asked her when he got back.

"Simon," she said, "here's how I remember them. Your mother was born first, so hers is on the twenty-first."

"You sure?"

"Pretty sure."

"But Diana is my first daughter. So maybe hers comes first."

"You're dripping. You look terrible. What happened to your knee?"

"I tripped on the hill down to Fifth. Cracks in the sidewalk, and it's steep there."

"And you weren't looking. Let me see that. Why didn't you come right back? Look, the blood ran down into your shoe."

"A guy on a motorcycle stopped. Asked me if I needed a ride home, but I said no. He was young and helpful-looking."

"And so?"

"And so, I told him thank you and that I was okay. I didn't need any help. I just wanted to keep running. It was no big deal. He was like twenty-five, and, all of a sudden, I felt like some old guy who should be home drinking tea and watching reruns of *Bonanza*. Anyway, I ran down to the Jackie Gleason Bus Depot and then back up the hill by the cemetery. That's like seven miles."

"You ran into Sunset Park and didn't bring back those good tacos?"

"I was bleeding."

"I'm just kidding."

"Tell me again, is tomorrow my mother's birthday or Diana's?"

"It's your mother's."

"I had a little trouble running back up the hill. Not because of my knee. I think my shoes are too heavy. Maybe I should get a lighter pair."

"Maybe you should go see a doctor. Your shoes don't, all of a sudden, get heavy."

"I noticed it first last week when I was pushing the stroller with the kids up Second Street to the park. I had to stop a couple of times."

"And you think it's because your shoes suddenly got too heavy?"

"That's how it felt."

"You should drink more water and make an appointment with Edelman. Maybe you should go tomorrow."

"I just ran seven miles. I really think I'm okay. I just need to train harder."

"Somehow that doesn't seem like a good plan."

"So, my mother's birthday is the twenty-first or the twenty-second. I'll try to remember that. It just seems not to stick in my head."

"Maybe it's just your shoes."

"Funny."

On the train, he didn't feel right. A bit tired. Anxious. Sweating. Proust was too hard to read. The run around the cemetery had been hard. Harder than he'd told Bernadette. His shoes were old, too heavy. You should buy new ones every six months, they say. Maybe it's every three months.

His chest was feeling tight. He took his jacket off. He stood up. He was beginning to feel panicky.

He needed to get off the train. Get out. Go someplace else. His heart was thudding. He could feel it in his head. Hear it in his ears. He felt as if he was going to die if he didn't get off the train.

At 50th Street, he took his things, left the train, and walked quickly across town to Saint Clare's. The ER was crowded with people. Old and young. Mothers with children. He walked up to the window. He told the woman there that he had chest pain. She told him to come in and sit down. He sat in a chair. He felt a shakiness he'd never felt before. Cold. Drained. He told the ER nurse he had chest pain. She asked him how severe. "A ten," he said.

"Let's take a look," she said, and he sat down in the chair next to her desk. She checked his pressure, listened to his heart. She picked up the phone. Held it to her ear. Punched in few numbers.

"What are you reading?" she asked him.

"*Swann's Way.*"

"Proust," she said, "heavy reading."

And then nothing. Total oblivion.

Nothing until he awoke and saw Bernadette standing by the bed, beside the IV pole.

"What happened?" he said.

"Well, for starters, you had a coronary right there in the ER, and they rushed you up or down or wherever it is to the cath lab. They put a stent in, and you're good to go."

"So I guess it wasn't my shoes."

"You didn't really think it was, did you?"

"I think I did. A little."

"So now, let's make a deal that on every July twenty-first, instead of having a heart attack, let's buy you a new pair of running shoes and a big chocolate cake with three candles on top and sing 'Happy Birthday' to your mother."

"Why three candles?"

"Well, one for your mother, one for Diana for the next day, and one for Marcel Proust, whose birthday is on the tenth and we always seem to forget it. Until he reminded us."

SLOANE

Her name was Sloane.

Her hair was long. A deep chestnut brown. She was tall. Her legs were a mile and a half long.

She leaned her head back against the doorframe of her small, sparse, kitchen and looked at him. She extended her arms toward him and gestured for him to come closer.

"Take your coat off," she said, "and fuck me." Her voice was a whisper.

A sudden flush of anticipation rushed through him. A swelling in the back of his throat. Heat warmed his chest. He went to her, sinking into her enveloping arms. She pressed herself close against him, and he followed her into the dimly lit bedroom. The only light in the room came from the lights of the marina along Oyster Bay. The only sound came from her breath in his ear.

They lay together as one body, rising and falling in swells and troughs as if in a dinghy moored in its place on the bay far below them.

There was more to him, though, than the mere physicality of being with her this first time. More than the sensual quiet of the room. More than the seeming endlessness of the hours. It was more than the elusive transcendent ecstatic freedom he felt, and yet, simultaneously, in some ways, it felt less to him. Less than with other women he had known. Even on a first meeting as this one was. There was something blank, something hidden in her ardor.

They had no prior history. He knew nearly nothing about her. No past hurts or flattering lies. No thought of consequences. No withholding. Nothing to hide. Or was there? No past superseding the present. This was only the moment. He was not phoning it in. No intrusive thoughts of bills to pay. No need to feign an early-morning dentist appointment. No words of love.

"Kiss my breasts again the way you did before," she said. And he did, and he again feathered the soft, slender downward slope of her narrow waist and up the rise of her hips. She exhaled softly, and he held her breath in his parted lips.

At some point he must have dozed off, though he could not recall when, and for a moment all he could think of was the mindless comfort of the last moment before he had been swallowed by sleep.

And then he heard her speaking. She was in another room. That is what had drawn him back into wakefulness. He sat up, pulled on his clothes, and carried his shoes into the kitchen. She was dressed. Her back was toward him. She hung up the phone and turned to him.

"I think you better leave," she said. "I'm sorry."

He had not heard the phone ring. He had been with her in her bed for hours, and now she gets a call? At three in the morning? Strange?

Not at all strange, he thought as he drove down the hill from the apartment she rented above the harbor, once he knew what was going on. She told him that she had a lover. The man was a doctor she worked with who, as she put it, was stuck in a weird and loveless marriage. A man she had tried to break up with because he wouldn't deal with his marriage problem, but who then called her or she called him at three in the morning because he said he could not live without her and could he see her once more and would do anything she asked him to. Anything.

When he left her apartment with the view of Oyster Bay and the lights of the sailboats and the stars, he knew that she would soon be pulling the other man to her and leaning her hips into his and they'd fall half-naked into her warm and rumpled bed as she had done with him. And he was oddly pleased by that thought and, truth be told, that he might, on some random Saturday night, receive a call from her and see her again, once more feeling the way he had felt that night.

Mason is at the stove, boiling water for tea. Mona has set out the toast, butter, and jam on the kitchen counter.

"I read your story," she says. "The one about Oyster Bay."

"Oyster Bay?" says Mason. "Is the English Breakfast okay for you?"

"Yes, thanks. The story that's six hundred seventy words long and in which you mention 'Oyster Bay,' or 'the bay,' or 'the marina' no less than six different times."

"It's not really about Oyster Bay. Do you want any milk in your tea?"

"Yes, thanks. Then I guess it needs a good edit, Mona says. "And, so how do you know this Sloane woman?"

"I don't know any Sloane woman. It's just a story I'm working on."

"A story? Since when do you write such stories? And what kind of a name is Sloane, anyway? And since when are you the Grand Poobah of Sex? 'Do I know this man?' I ask myself. This man who writes 'fuck me' stories? Is this the Mason I married and who I love? The man who understands how terribly women are demeaned, devalued, and wantonly objectified. Who respects women? Who makes me tea in the afternoon?"

"It's a story, Mona. Nothing more. It's a first draft."

"Story, schmory. Who am I to think this Sloane woman is supposed to be? This poor woman in your dreams with legs a mile and a half long? And what does that mean, anyway? Have you thought about that? This poor woman is victimized. She needs to get some clarity about her situation and the choices she has made in her life. How she gets herself into relationships that have nowhere to go and which keep her dependent upon the whims and desires of some self-centered schmuck who only wants to schtup her at three o'clock in the morning when he should be home with his wife being straight with her, because he's screwing her over, too, in a very different and hateful way. She shouldn't be with another random guy who is content, to prey upon her again if she would let him. And this is what you write about?"

"I..."

"What am I to think, Mason, when I read this story? Which, by the way, is sloppy and superficial. With no plot and no tension? It's a piece of pandering, self-serving, uncritical, poorly written, thoughtless trash. Think about it, Mason. You're only perpetuating the same hateful objectification of women that has been at the heart of the male-privileged, male-fantasy-satisfying, leering, misogynistic, porn-fried world we live in."

"Mona."

"Don't 'Mona' me, and please, whatever you do, Mason, don't put this totally adolescent dime-store pulp-fiction drivel out there where anyone with an ounce of grace, respect, and humanity can read it."

"Your tea is getting cold. I know it's bad. The story. You're right, it needs a lot of work. I'm not sure yet where it's going?"

"No? Well, I have a good suggestion of where it might go."

THE SEVEN GOLDEN CITIES OF CIBOLA

The house lights dim. The screen behind the stage fades from black to a cerulean, a white *C* in the center. A spotlight is on Diego Coronado walking to center stage. He looks like an eighteen-year-old swimmer, but he's got to be fifty, at least.

"I got one question," says Phil, "whose ass did he have to kiss to get this job?" *This is my friend Phil, sitting next to me. Sometimes he can be a severely negative dickhead.*

"The hell are you talking about?" *This is me.*

"I don't know. I just heard things."

"You just heard things? That's bullshit. His father owns the company. He worked at Goldman. Morgan Stanley. He knows his shit."

"I didn't say he doesn't know his shit. Just sayin' he might have risen to a level a bit beyond his abilities."

"Maybe he did. Or maybe you're just being a dickhead."

We stand. Clapping until Coronado raises his hand.

"Gentlemen. Ladies. Others." *This is Coronado.*

"Twenty generations ago, Francisco de Coronado, my great-grandfather many times over, then the governor of Nueva Galicia, several hundred miles south of here, learned of the Seven Golden Cities of Cibola.

"Blinded by the prospect of enormous wealth, he led three hundred of his men and a thousand Native Americans, likely captured slaves, hundreds of miles north, killing and looting Zuni villages only to find nothing of what he sought.

"He returned home to Compostela, poor, injured, and ridiculed. He'd seen the Grand Canyon, the Colorado River, the Rio Grande. They were not good enough. He wanted gold. He risked everything and he lost everything."

The room got quiet. Coronado looked at us. A roomful of men and women. All not-so-secretly seeking the wealth of which he spoke.

"What do *you* want? What do *you* seek? What will *you* risk? For what? For *happiness*? For *gold*?"

He was speaking to me. To all of us. Hundreds of us. Brokers. Managing directors. VPs.

"Coronado Capital Management employs thirty-one thousand hardworking people like you. Our largest cost center is salaries, benefits, and bonuses. The average annual employee makes around thirty-five hundred K. Some managing directors make eight figures. Last quarter, that single expense line was close to 2.9 billion."

"Holy crap. That's a shitload of beans!" *This is Phil.*

"Add to that rent, renovations, debt service, IT, PR, communications, travel, training, advertising, and interest, and our operating expenses top twenty-five billion. With net revenues of thirty billion, we run lean. With 2001 and 2008 and who knows what 2020 or beyond will bring, we need to run leaner."

"You smell some doo-doo about to hit the fan?" *Phil again.*

"Putting money aside for a minute. Are we happy? Are you happy?" *Coronado*

Murmuring spreads. Scattered coughing. Butts shift in their seats.

"Remember Maslow's hierarchy of needs? Food, water, shelter. A job. Personal security? Friendship? Self-esteem? Self-actualization? Maslow said, 'What a person can be, he must be.' Are you being the person you can and want to be? What are you putting off? When was the last time you hit a baseball or went to the beach without your Blackberry? Read a great book? Thought thoughts you never get time to think? Had nothing to do with work or money or taxes or obligations? Are you the person you can be? I will give you the chance to be that person."

Silence.

"Marx once said, 'Money is the alienated essence of man's work and existence: this essence dominates him and he worships it.' Is this what we all have become?"

"Marx?" *Phil*

"Shut up, Phil."

"Ninety percent of adults spend half their lives doing things they would rather not be doing at places they would rather not be. Know anybody like that? At Coronado, you and I together can change that. Not the world maybe, but ourselves."

He crosses the stage.

"We are overcapitalized. We are in debt to our debt. My guess is that you are too. Debt is the killer. It makes us take risks we should not take. But...there is a way out."

The walls are being washed in light the color of the Mediterranean.

"Welcome to the Coronado of tomorrow! With our cash on hand, we will pay off our debt. Pull all services inside. Buy what we need with cash. No more rent or mortgages on underused out-of-date office buildings. We will self-insure. We will owe no one anything. *And*, we will continue to be the same Coronado the financial world depends upon.

"How do we do this? What's in it for you? The company will pay for your home wherever you want, a car, your club membership, your food bills, vacations, everything you need. You do your job, but you get no salary, no bonuses."

"What the fuck?" *Phil, again.*

"You won't need any of that. Coronado will pay for everything. You work remotely. You continue to produce A+ work and you will own your own labor. Your own life. Coronado takes the burden, the worry, and risk of debt off of you. You will be debt- and risk-free. And, when you retire, you'll get a great pension for the rest of your life. The company cuts its costs, lowers its risk, pays dividends, and you get a life truly worth living. If we can pull this off, it will change the nature of work and possibly the nature of humanity."

"I'm in!" *This me shouting. Standing. I'm imbued with the spirit.* "This guy is fantastic!"

"Whoa!" *This is Phil.* "You're in? You're in? Who's the dickhead now? You believe this bullshit? This Coronado dude is feeding you a hook in a hot dog. Marxism in a meatball. He's a commie-capitalist chameleon. What's his game? Shilling for a suburban slavery ring? You think he's not going to get rich off this brain-free deal?"

Phil gets up, squeezing past the row of standing, cheering men and women, their hands raised high.

"When you're all done with this circle jerk, drop me a line from your yurt in the Urals, goofball!" *Phil again, heading toward the door.*

I sit down. "Yo, Phil...where are you going?"

"You can stay, but I'm getting out when I can. When I can still enjoy the freedom of being just an ordinary capitalist tool!"

The Mime and the Money

Peter Pindar takes his usual seat on the southbound 7:28 a.m. Metro North train at Croton-Harmon. He has silver-gray hair and wears a notched-lapel, two-button, double-vented, indigo-blue Armani suit, a white flare collar, and a four-in-hand green tie. He nods hello to the two gentlemen across the aisle. The men nod back. He places his monthly ticket under the clip on the seat back.

At Ossining, the conductor taps his shoulder. "Expired."

"Beg pardon?"

"Your ticket. It's a new month. You need a new one."

"Goodness," says Pindar. "Doesn't that beat all?"

"That'll be $14 one way to Grand Central, or I'm sorry, Mr. P, but I'll have to put you off at Phillips Manor."

"What an embarrassment. You know me, Glen," Pindar whispers. "Would a personal note suffice? I'm a tad short today, and I will certainly show you my new card on Monday."

The train pulls even with the platform at Phillips Manor, the last stop before it goes express to 125th Street.

"Look," the conductor says, snapping off a fresh receipt, "this could mean my job."

Pindar hands him his business card: Peter Pindar, Manager, Tourneau Corner, Fine Watches, 200 W 34th Street. "Thank you," he says. "Your kindness knows no bounds."

From Grand Central, Pindar walks south, breathing in the fresh city air, breathing out his troubles. His heels click on the pavement along Madison.

At the corner of 34th and Broadway, the familiar fading shop window sign reads: "This Tourneau has permanently closed. Please visit our new Bryant Park location."

No surprise. He knows Swarovski will be moving in.

At the curb, he buys a coffee, light and sweet.

"Good day, Mr. P," the vendor smiles.

Pindar walks uptown to 42nd Street, finds a chair in the Rose Reading Room at the library, and unfolds the copy of the *Journal* he picked up at the recycling bin as he left the train.

At noon, Pindar folds the paper under his arm and takes the rear doors out to Bryant Park. People are sitting in chairs, some around tables, eating lunch, taking in the sun.

In one corner of the well-trimmed lawn, a small crowd encircles a mime in whiteface, top hat, striped shirt, and bell-bottoms. Pindar joins the circle and claps joyfully at the mime's every move.

When the mime asks for a volunteer to come join him, Pindar is the first to raise his hand. But then when the thin mime gestures for him to come join him in the center, Pindar waves him off, embarrassed by the attention. The mime insists. The onlookers insist.

"Go ahead, go ahead!" they insist.

Pindar hands the folded *Journal* to one of his fellow onlookers and stands stiffly beside the mime. There is warm applause. Pindar bows.

He and the mime look out to the audience, and at the mime's urging, Pindar turns to face him, watching his every move. Slowly, almost in tandem, their eyes close and open as if seeing their own reflection in a mirror. They lean toward each other. The mime touches his left cheek, and Pindar touches his right. For seven solid minutes, they move in nearly flawless manikin-like unison.

When they are done, they both bow low. The crowd roars. Children rush to drop coins and dollar bills in the mime's top hat.

"You were so brave and wonderful. You look like you do this all the time," a young woman in a pink dress pats him on the shoulder. "I could never have done that in a million years."

He is embarrassed and nods, looking away from her.

He is flushed and famished, and retrieves the *Journal,* buys a hot dog, and sits at a table in the shade.

A couple walk by and give him the thumbs up. He smiles back at them.

At three fifteen, a gentleman in a gray suit and tie, gestures to ask if he may sit at Pindar's table. They do not speak. The man slips an envelope into the folded newspaper and leaves. Pindar picks up the paper, removes the envelope, and slips it into his breast pocket. He taps it to feel its thickness.

At a pay phone at the edge of the park, he calls home and leaves a message for his wife on their answering machine.

"Marguerite, dear, our sales at the store were slow for a Friday. I left Eduardo and Glenda to close up shop, and I'll be taking the 4:53 home. I cashed a check, and I bought the paper for you. I'll pick up a seeded rye at Zaro's."

Precisely on time, Pindar salutes as he passes beneath Coulan's sculpture of Mercury, the god of travel and commerce, which is flanked by Hercules and Minerva atop the entrance to Grand Central Terminal. He makes his way to Gate 37 and takes the silver city express to Croton-Harmon, showing the conductor the round-trip receipt from the morning train.

"You have a good weekend, Mr. P."

I had been staying with a group of friends in a small room in a rather large hotel in a warm climate during the year following the death of my father. The room was on the second floor of the hotel, though sometimes it was on the fifth floor. In either case, it was in an older section of the hotel and one that had not yet undergone the elaborate renovations that were made in the finer and more expensive sections.

I say "section" because the hotel seemed to be divided into clearly separate areas or towers, each with a large outdoor pool and a well-appointed dining room. The elevators in each of these areas served only the upper floors of each particular tower.

Expansive clear glass French doors gave entrance to each section on the main floor, which was the floor above the lobby, which itself was open to the public as lobbies need to be. But entry into the pools, dining areas, and upper floors was limited to those guests and residents of the tower in which they were registered, and access was monitored—though, at times, I was seemingly able to pass through from one area to another unimpeded, as it may have been that I was unnoticed or innocuous and pedestrian enough to be treated as though I were not there. I must note, though, that I was not aware of or simply could not remember when or under what circumstances I came to be a guest of the hotel. Nor do I know for what reason, if any, or how long I had been there.

When I actually had occasion to pass from one area of the hotel to another, as often was the case, searching for the elevator to the older and shabbier section of the hotel in which the room I shared with my friends could be found, I was certain that I was being watched and, moreover, feared being stopped and questioned about where I was going and what my room number was.

This was a prospect that frightened me, since at no time was I certain of either the floor or the number of the room in which my things were kept, and I never was in possession of a room key. I believed, too, that we were all being closely watched and that distinctions among the guests and the privileges to which they were entitled varied greatly on the basis, I assumed, of social class and apparent wealth, though I had no firm evidence upon which I had come to that belief.

At no time, other than the exact moment at which I departed my room, and I carefully examined the black painted number on the wine-dark door and attempted to memorize it, was I remotely able to conjure the floor or the room number or even the direction along the dim corridor, which was configured in a complete square, where my room could be found upon exiting the elevator. There was, of course, due to fire regulations, an interior staircase that gave access to all of the floors. It was less and less ornate as it rose to the upper floors of the section that contained my room.

More disconcerting, however, was the construction of the little-used stairway in this older section of the hotel, as there were portions that led one through what may have been a labyrinth of passageways for maintenance staff, as they were crowded with ducts and pipes bound in gray insulation padding. Of great diameter and variety, they ran through the staircase at angles, causing one to squeeze under or over them and to step or to be forced to leap across open shaftways or to walk along the narrow gray-painted ledges along the openings to reach the entry to the next level of the staircase. Similarly, in the lowest levels of the staircase, which was well-lighted and appeared to be gold-plated, one would come to a point where the stairs were blocked by a filigreed latticework that did not communicate directly to the stairs either below or above, depending on the direction in which you were headed and which required one to climb, once again, over and up or down to reach the next level. At times, it was not possible for me to make my way down to the next level, and I found I had to exit through a side doorway onto a path that led to parking lots and tall buildings, such as one might encounter in an urban commercial center and through which I had to find my way back around to the main entrance of the hotel.

Despite this anomalous exterior, there were sunny white dunes just outside of the window of the room I shared with these friends, whose names I did not know and which I believe I had never been told. My belongings were strewn around the mattress on the floor upon which I slept, though I could not recall ever actually sleeping on it. My suitcase was at the bottom of a stack of similar-looking cases that likely belonged to the three or four others.

My cell phone was among the few possessions that I had carried with me to the hotel, but when I left my room, I often found myself without it, perhaps having forgotten it in the room. At times, I found it in my pocket with a useless, dead battery. And, though on the occasion when I found the phone with some charge remaining on it and saw the opportunity to call home, I could not recall the phone number, since I had long forgotten the number of the home I grew up in and seemed to confuse it with the number of my ex-wife's cell phone and therefore could reach neither her nor my long-dead mother.

The high dunes that I could see clearly outside through my room's only window created a barrier between the hotel and the open ocean. When the tide was up and the winds blew from offshore, we could see the waves, which must have been thirty feet in height, peak and plunge over the tall dunes and flood the narrow space along the exterior of the building. We would crowd around the window, some of us standing on one of the beds closest to the window, to see how high the waves would get and how much water would fill the moat, though none of us seemed concerned at all that the monstrous waves would crash through the flimsy, ill-fitting window.

The excitement of the peaking waves had us all calling out loudly, "This is the one!" or "Oh, God, this is it!" and then as soon as the waves receded, I would find myself out on the placid beach, having hiked through a narrow path over the dunes to where the sunbathers—mostly older, portly men and women on lounge chairs with darkly tanned and weathered skin—sat with glasses of iced tea in their hands. They pointed me to the farthest end of the beach where the younger guests could be seen both in the waves and on the shore, including my roommates and several very attractive young women they seemed to be friendly with.

One of these, a lithe, long-legged woman with a narrow waist and long dark hair folded neatly in a bun at the nape of her neck, stood so close and seductively next to me that I assumed we were somehow coupled, though at no time did that play out in anything more than a fleeting adolescent fantasy of mine. I must admit that the prospect of something more was never far from my thoughts, though, in truth, they had never coalesced into anything more than the vaguest of sexual possibility. And at that very moment, I would find myself alone once again with a shuddering suddenness, back in the hotel searching my mind and my surroundings simultaneously and fruitlessly for the floor and the number of the room I shared with the others, as well as the correct staircase or elevator to use, and my phone with which to call my mother or my wife, only to find myself, without any agency on my part, somehow inside the unlocked and empty room, which had been abandoned by the group of young men I believed I had shared the space with. So at once, without concern or deliberation, I turned and ventured out into the hallway, once again allowing the door to close tightly behind me.

Forest Pike at the
Old House on Main Street

Forest Pike parked his car behind the senior center at the south end of Main Street, across from the house being renovated. It had long been left sadly without upkeep, the white-painted wood clapboard siding exposed in large bare patches, and the windows sagging on the north side though none had been broken. In the years he had lived in town he had never known anyone to live there.

He'd been watching the impeachment hearings on CNN. They were droning on, men and women in suits, standing up and buttoning their neat jackets and saying mostly what they'd been saying all day, all week, all year, with charts and quotes and apologies for their repetition. Though, what new could they say? Nothing had changed. Nothing was going to.

He'd turned the set off when one of the speakers was earnestly in mid-sentence. *No disrespect,* he thought. He didn't want to hear what Blitzer or Toobin or Maddow would say. He didn't want to hear what that fool Dershowitz would say. Nor what Susan Collins or Mitt had to say. He'd heard enough from them all.

So he just laced up his sneakers, put on his jacket, and headed over to work out on one of the treadmills the town had put in for retirees. He'd sweat for thirty or forty minutes and go home for lunch.

He thought he'd just seen about everything there was to see in this town. A town with an unyielding dearth of novelty. Little predilection or openness to change. A town from which, when the weather was right and you squinted your eyes a little, you could see, across the water, the thin gray line of the coast of Maine. A town without a stoplight. A town that attracted busloads of tourists, whose willing cash paid for parking, sweatshirts, and lobster rolls, and whose jaywalking, selfies, garish dress, and inability to parallel park incensed the locals. Tourists who paid a high price to see a place that more resembled a postcard, which led them to believe that it *was* a postcard image created for their use rather than a real place with real people living there.

So the house being renovated across from the senior center got the townspeople talking. The word was that someone from the city had bought it as a teardown like the houses built by the water. They'd raze it, and in its stead, given that it was located in the historic district, put up a house very much like it, except that it would be more house than anyone might need, for more money than most people had, and would cut off the view of the neighbors across the way who'd paid good money for the view of the headlands forty years before.

No, the townspeople did not like change. But some changes were tolerated, others not. Tax money from the big houses paid for a lot of new trucks and machinery for pothole repair and new police cruisers. But property values increased and affordable housing was always too much of a change. The mere mention of it brought up questions of appropriateness or need. Of overburdening the sewer system or preserving wetland.

There was complaining at town meeting when the dry laws were threatened or when the liberals started carping about sanctuary cities, and the conservatives raised specters of brown-skinned illegals carrying drugs and malice, amassing at the town line waiting for the chance to invade.

The house on Main had not gotten torn down. Most likely, the zoning board—or maybe it was the historical commission—had their say. And so, when Forest parked his car, he saw that the old house, its clapboard siding stripped bare to reveal stained hundred-year-old boards, was up on ten-foot wooden pilings. You could see clear through underneath it with the whole of the old place up in the air and only those stilts holding it up. He figured they would be building the new part of the house right there under the old one and make it look like nothing had changed, except that over the weekend when most folks were eating corn chips waiting for the Super Bowl to start, the house would get ten feet taller with a new first floor and a paint job to match the old paint job.

That's the way it was in the town.

There was a sign up in front of the house up on stilts, a hand-lettered sign on a square of brown cardboard. It said "Keep Out."

The sign put him in mind of a sign on a similar piece of brown cardboard he saw some years back in a painting at a friend's place, back when he lived in Brooklyn. In the painting, there was a man whose age you couldn't be sure of sitting on a sidewalk, as you'd see all over the city then, his back up against a brick wall with some graffiti scrawled on it. His face was creased with woe and dark with urban grime. The brown cardboard sign he held in his lap said "Keep your coins...I want change."

You and me both, buddy, Forest thought. It was himself he could see in the painting. He had always been waiting for change. Waiting for a semblance of justice, compassion, regard.

The things he had seen. Internment, relocation, Auschwitz, McCarthy, Selma, Tuskegee, Vietnam, Nixon, the Kennedys, King, Evers, nukes, Iran-Contra, Iraq, Afghanistan, Iran, Trayvon. Truth bleeding out in the middle of the streets. The succession of all of that. It seemed never to stop. The same cold, lifeless bodies, arms splayed out, simply dressed in different clothes. The migrants in endless lines, the jails filled with tossed-off souls and ruined lives. *My God,* he thought, *will I ever live to see change?*

Why did the house up on stilts set him off like this?

It was not the house or the town. It was the totality of it all. The constancy of breaking news that was breaking him.

The raised-up house on wooden stilts had become the wooden desk above his head in the grade-school atomic bomb drills. The crass, lying, bald-faced futility of it. To keep you from thinking about why there were bombs falling from the skies at all. The poorly disguised deceit offered up just to keep it all the same, looking the same. Raising alarms at something to make it seem new rather than the old story that it was. The "look what's coming at us now!" The new conjured enemy that we needed to sacrifice for in order to be defended by military force. The new thing to fear and hate.

The thing is, Forest thought, *nobody with the power to make change wants things to change.* We are destined, as Plato might have said, to be forever ruled by evil men or fools—or both.

He removed the key from the ignition, got out of the car, and walked not toward the senior center but across the street toward the house in the fine drizzle that had started. He slipped under the strip of curled yellow warning tape and stepped down into the space below the house. He stood on the freshly turned russet-colored earth in the bare, excavated vault under the old house and imagined how, if the wind blew hard enough or if there was a well-placed blow to the weakest strut, the old house might shift just enough off of its tired stilts and fall like a slow, whining bomb upon his bent and worried gray head.

The Precipice and the Wild Strawberries

"Mom, where's Dad?"

"I sent him to the market."

"It's ten o'clock. He shouldn't be out this late. I would have gone for you. What did you need so late?"

"Strawberries."

"Strawberries?"

"Yes. Can't a person have strawberries when they want them? Is that such a sin?"

"But at ten o'clock, in the rain? He'll miss Don Lemon."

"There are more important things in life than Don Lemon, you know."

"But—"

"Don't 'but' me. Besides, all he ever does when he's watching Don Lemon—which, by the way, is not really like watching the news anymore—is satisfying his confrontation bias, according to Aunt Ethel."

"Ethel said that? Confrontation bias? Isn't it confirmation bias?"

"No, Ethel says when her Milton watches CNN, he gets all worked up and it's like he's looking for a fight. She has to make him a glass of Lights Out! Sleepytime Tea with a little peach schnapps in it so she can live with him till he falls asleep in his chair."

"But Dad is not like that."

"Malachi. You don't live with him. Your father thinks the world is crumbling around him. He talks to the television. 'Oh my God,' he says. 'Australia, and sea level, the Democrats. And Putin. Mitch McConnell, Iran, all ready. Coronavirus. We're doomed,' he says. 'Harold,' I tell him, 'calm down. Take a cleansing breath and put a mask on.' So I sent him out for strawberries."

"Why?"

"To help him deal with doom. Your sister Felicia said I should do it. She's a Buddhist now, you know. She takes classes at the Y in the evening."

"A Buddhist? She takes classes at the Y and that makes her a Zen Buddhist? I thought she was an agnostic."

"She is. She says she's searching for her own path to enlightenment. And I don't think it's a Buddhist kind of Zen. I think it is a special Jewish kind of Zen."

"And strawberries are on the path to Zen Jewish enlightenment?"

"Yes. She told me the teacher told them a very important Zen Cohen story."

"Ma? What is a Zen Cohen story?"

"Cohen, I said, like your uncle Henry, the optician. Anyway, don't interrupt me. Just listen to me. You will learn something. The Zen Cohen story is about a woman who is walking through the Prospect Park Zoo one day and a ferocious tiger escapes from its cage and starts chasing her."

"There are no tigers in the Prospect Park Zoo."

"Please, Malachi, put both your feet on the floor, close your mouth, and open your mind. It's philosophy. So this tiger is chasing her. She runs as fast as she can, but she comes to a sharp precipice over by Flatbush Avenue where there's all that construction, and it's like fifty feet deep all the way down, so she looks to her right and looks to her left, and there's nowhere else to run, no escape, except...

"Except what?"

"Except over the edge. She just steps right over the edge of the cliff, and it's after four o'clock and all the workers and people have gone home and it's January and it's almost dark and, as she's going over the precipice, she grabs onto the only thing she can see, a really thick vine growing out of the dirt on the side of the cliff, and she is saved from the tiger, except..."

"Except what?"

"Except that she sees all the way down at the bottom of the cliff is another tiger. Another tiger that somehow escaped from the tiger cage, and it is looking up at her and waiting for her to fall so it can eat her. *Disaster,* right? And if that was not enough, right there on the vine, closest to the side, are these two big, ugly, gray subway rats from the F train, big as porcupines, sticking their heads out of a hole and gnawing away at the vine and, sure as New York knishes are round, they are going to cut clear through it in a minute. She is doomed. And then...and then, out of the corner of her eye, she sees just within her reach a plump, juicy, red wild strawberry growing right there on the vine in front of her, and..."

"And what?"

"And she grabs for the strawberry!"

"She's going to die, and she grabs for the strawberry? That's it?"

"That's it."

"You eat a damn strawberry and then you get eaten by a tiger? That's it? That's the whole point?"

"Yes. Felicia says the Zen Cohen means that you have to take whatever joy out of life you can whenever it comes your way because you never know. You could step off the curb tomorrow and get hit by the B37 bus. So you should grab it while you can."

"And that story is supposed to calm your mind? I'd rather have a cup of Lights Out with a shot of peach schnapps and a little sugar like Milton."

"You don't get it."

"Mom, I get it. But grabbing at all the joy when you can doesn't mean you send your husband down to 7th Avenue at ten o'clock at night across busy 9th Street to buy strawberries at the corner deli.

And, by the way, I'm sure Felicia didn't say it's a Zen Cohen. It's not Jewish. It's a *koan. K-O-A-N.* It's a Japanese Buddhist Zen koan that is on the path to enlightenment."

"Koan, schmoan. I should worry. You're missing the point."

"No, Ma, I know you meant well, but you're the one missing the point. And Dad is missing Don Lemon. Why don't you just let him pick his own strawberries in life?"

Silence.

PROLOGUE TO
BEING AND NOTHINGNESS

Jean-Paul had no classes to teach on Thursdays. On those days, he had coffee in the late morning at one or another of the cafés he frequented. He'd then read and write all afternoon, meeting with Simone and the others in the evening for dinner. On that one November Thursday morning, the eighth, there was a thickened, ominous atmosphere of imminent war within the café on Rue de Bretagne, as there was in all of Paris.

It had been raining since Monday. The sidewalks of Paris were gray, covered with a slurry of footprints and sodden cigarette butts.

Sartre brought his coffee and a sweet pastry to a table in the rear. He draped his coat over the chair beside him. Favoring his privacy, he avoided conversation with those he didn't know. He sat with his back to the entrance. Unfolded his newspaper.

The picture of a young man was on the front page. The man was in police custody. An officer was holding him by the arm.

He was a young Jew with dark, thick eyebrows. It was the first thing Sartre noticed about him. There was a sallow furtiveness in his face. Lidded eyes; a foreign sharp line to his features. His hands were in the pockets of a light overcoat. He wore a tie and a three-piece gray suit. He was seventeen, the paper said. His name was Herschel Grynszpan.

Grynszpan had been arrested by the French authorities for shooting Ernst vom Rath, a mid-level functionary in the German embassy, on the day before. Surrounding him in the photo were several men, all much taller than he, guiding him, it seemed, as he passed through a narrow, open doorway in the police headquarters.

Sartre knew that the boy would be subjected to the harshest of punishment. He knew the Germans well. An example, no doubt, would be made of him. The Reich, he thought, would not let this pass.

The boy and his situation intrigued him. A boy of seventeen? Moved, at the risk of almost assured death, to shoot this one man? A man he did not know. Why had he not spent the day working or walking by the river and eating fruit and candies?

The authorities had found a note, a postcard, in the boy's pocket, addressed to his parents: "With God's help. My dear parents, I could not do otherwise, may God forgive me, the heart bleeds when I hear of your tragedy and that of the 12,000 Jews. I must protest so that the whole world hears my protest, and that I will do. Forgive me."

Sartre picked up the paper and left the café. He could not clear his thoughts of what he had read. As he walked home, he imagined what it would be like if *he* had shot the man. If *he* himself had bought the revolver and pulled the trigger, feeling its jarring recoil each of the five times it was fired. Smelling the cordite. Seeing the blood spurt from the other man's abdomen. Feeling the oily residue on his fingers.

He searched the papers each morning to learn more about this young man. This Herschel.

On November 9, the night following the shooting, Joseph Goebbels, in Munich, called for reprisals, enflaming German youth to run through the streets to hunt down Jews, to riot and beat them. To smash the windows of their shops, to loot, to rape women in their homes.

Broken glass littered the streets. Thousands of synagogues throughout Germany and Austria were set afire by the SA, the paramilitary Sturmabteilung. Twenty thousand Jews were arrested. Sent to Dachau and Buchenwald and Sachsenhausen. Hundreds were killed where they stood.

Sartre knew vom Rath's death had been only a pretext for the deadly pogroms, the premeditated rampaging violence unleashed in the immediate aftermath of a waited-for precipitating event.

Herschel, Sartre wrote in his notebook later, could not have known what the aftermath would be. No doubt, Sartre thought, the boy must have been prepared to die. He had acted alone. With no thought of an outcome or consequence. No thought beyond the single act. No greater plan than to act.

The boy had been sent to Paris by his parents to live with his uncle. To save him. Already, in 1938, there was no hope that any Polish Jew stripped of Polish citizenship and deported to Germany without any papers would survive. In Paris there was hope. In Paris though, he had not found freedom. With no papers, he could get no job. He wandered the streets, reciting poetry. He slept in hiding.

And then, on the morning of November 7, with a little over 200 francs he had taken from his uncle, Herschel bought a 6.35 mm revolver on the Rue du Faubourg Saint-Martin and walked to the German embassy at 78 Rue de Lille. Along the Seine. Asking there to see the German ambassador. Seeing instead an assistant. Vom Rath.

After the shooting, Herschel gave his name to the authorities. He had neither resisted nor tried to escape.

The look on Herschel's face, what he had done, his fate, haunted Sartre.

He wrote of the boy in his diaries throughout the occupation, then during his time in the French army, and after he was captured, in all the time he spent in a German prisoner-of-war camp.

When he had time to think and write, he thought of the boy. Of the boy's "situation," as he called it, and of the boy's singular act of what Sartre would later call "contingency violence." A willful act. An act of being.

What is it to be free? he thought.

France was not free. The boy was not free. He was not free. All there was, all there ever was left to a person, was the ability to act on one's behalf, and through that there was the hope of freedom.

The meaning of *being,* Sartre wrote, was *being-for-oneself.* To act in one's own situation is the act of *being.* Of *existence.* Of *freedom.*

To not act for oneself, to be complacent, and to accept that complacency as all there is left to you in life, a situation to be endured in a sense of powerlessness, even with fear and anger, he wrote, is *nothingness.*

Circumflexion

Adelaide Molloy worked seventeen dutiful years in the employ of Abraham, Isaacs & Jacobson, attorneys at law. As had her sister, Millie, before she'd left the firm unexpectedly and moved back down south and opened an adult video store near Orlando, where the two sisters had grown up. She'd used the proceeds from a lucrative separation package—likely, Adelaide expected, the result of the revelation of an affair with one of the partners or the exposure of unethical behavior involving a client.

Adelaide herself was a smart, assiduously ethical, and meticulously rigorous research assistant. Uncompromisingly dedicated to the firm. She was well compensated, secure, and able to afford a comfortable fourth-floor walk-up on Carroll Street in Brooklyn, just above Fifth.

An adequate amateur runner, she ran the NYC marathon twice with the AI&J charity team, raising over $150,000 for the Presbyterian Hospital burn unit.

She worked long hours, took reams of work home, went to bed late, and woke up early. She watched her back. She enjoyed her good fortune but never took it for granted. She lived with her mother's constant admonition: *Don't be a fool, Adelaide, nothing good ever comes from good fortune. Never will. And if it comes, it will soon be gone.*

On one hot July day, Adelaide's mother proved to be remarkably and pointedly prescient.

On her way to work that morning on the subway, which was stalled over the Gowanus Canal, Adelaide had a minor run-in with another passenger.

As Adelaide stood, holding the handrail above the seats, a fellow passenger, a woman wearing several layers of overcoats and a pair of Gucci sunglasses, looked up and said to Adelaide, who had been lost in thought and a bit queasy, having slept badly the night before, "The fuck you looking at? You think you better than me, bitch?"

Adelaide felt trapped; she couldn't breathe. She turned away from the woman, taking a seat in another part of the car. The woman continued haranguing her from across the car until the woman gathered her bags and left the train at Jay Street.

Adelaide felt unwell. She felt trapped. Confined. She had felt this way before. Confrontation, discord, and judgment all brought the feeling on. Growing up, that was all there was at home. Her parents fought. Worse than that. And now there was this sad, frightening, awful woman.

Instead of going to the office, she walked to the health clinic near St. Vincent's and was seen by a young doctor, who ordered an EKG.

The results showed nothing untoward, and when Adelaide asked for some medication for anxiety, he told her he couldn't prescribe her any without doing a full psych exam, instructing her to go home, breathe into a paper bag, and go to the ER if her symptoms persisted.

Which they did,' and which Adelaide did.

Later in the day, she left home and walked the ten blocks to the New York-Presbyterian Brooklyn Methodist Hospital ER. They brought her into an exam room. She was frightened and agreed to have an emergency cardiac catheterization.

When she woke up in recovery, they told her, they had found a narrowing in her left coronary circumflex artery. The one that branches into the left anterior descending artery and into the thick muscle of her heart. The stent they snaked into her artery should do the job, she was good, they said, and she was released several days later.

Well, the job itself had *not* been good. Far from good. What, exactly though, was not good, the hospital was a bit vague about. They had refused to say any more.

It was only through her own thorough review of the medical notes of each of the surgeons and nurses and an audio tape of the procedure that she had obtained, that she discovered that the coronary stent and the balloon catheter had become trapped while crossing the angulated segment between the left circumflex and left main coronary artery, and the balloon had become stripped from the stent. The balloon had to be forcibly removed by an unorthodox trans-catheter maneuver resulting in tearing of the arterial wall, causing the potential for an aneurism to develop at some time in the future. It had been a rare but avoidable complication, but nothing an experienced cardiac cath team couldn't handle.

The point, though, which Adelaide learned from the surgical audiotape, was that the interventional cardiologist had become flustered and flummoxed and defensively ignored the team's advice.

Adelaide was devastated. Violated. *Had the rushed surgery even been warranted in the first place?*

With the data in hand, Adelaide spoke in confidence to Arnie Abraham, the senior partner of AI&J and a close friend, who told her she had a good case against Presbyterian. A very good case.

She wanted to be made whole again. She was heartened.

Temporarily.

But AI&J, Arnie continued, could not take her case. They represented Presbyterian in medical malpractice claims and had lost only a single case in forty-three years. They could not lose another.

Bernard Iskowitz, the security officer, helped Adelaide to the elevator door with her coat and belongings, leaving neither an opportunity for goodbyes nor a warm, consoling cup of tea. Her computer passwords had already been changed and her files encrypted. A deposit of a half million dollars in cash was made in her bank account. Severance. *What a terrible word,* she thought.

With Millie's help, Adelaide filed suit.

Arnie called her. Told her to drop it. To settle. She didn't.

She lost. Not a soul from the hospital would testify on her behalf. She appealed. She lost again.

She felt wrecked and wretched and moved in with Millie over the video store in Orlando. She made friends there. Shared her story with a few empathetic folks she trusted and tried to put the whole thing behind her.

To no avail.

She was relentlessly enraged. Increasingly consumed with anger and a bleeding desire for revenge. She could see herself, *feel* herself, beating Arnie, the surgeon, and the judge, about the back and shoulders with a tire iron. Pounding hard against their ribs, their flailing arms. Though, of course, she told herself, she would never do that.

Arnie had betrayed her. She had a potentially fatal aneurism as a result of a botched operation. He covered it up. He knew better. He hung her out to dry. Somewhere along the line, he would have to pay for what had been done to her.

Time went on. She made subtle inquiries, was given names and numbers.

She met a gentleman on a sandy beach north of Delray through someone who knew someone who knew someone, without a single real name being exchanged. He said he could help her out. His name, he said, was Sedge. He said he had once worked as a corrections officer up north, in Jersey, in another life. He knew people. He had connections he could trust.

Sedge was a good guy. He had a kind and caring heart. She trusted him.

She gave him a considerable sum of cash, which he said he would not take for himself but would pass along. He told her that her Arnie problem would one day be taken care of. She had nothing to worry about. No one would ever be able to connect her to anything.

They walked along the beach. Sedge was well tanned. He smelled of lemongrass. The sun glancing off his shoulders gleamed in her eyes. She'd never be made whole again, she knew, but there would be a measure of retribution. Life, her life, would be better.

FISHMAN THE FOOL

Marvin Fishman and Darlene Meriwether broke up. She called him a fool. A loser. A leech.

Actually, she told him , "You're a forty-two-year-old divorced loser with no job, no money, no prospects, living in Malvern, Long Island, in a four-bedroom center-hall colonial with his mother and a cat that lives in the basement and pees in her plants. What kind of a person does that? A loser and a fool."

Up till then, they had dated on and off. But then, that evening, over a bowl of vegetable jalfrezi she had made from scratch, he said he thought he just didn't think he'd ever get married again.

Her face fell.

Only moments before, she had said maybe it was time for him to turn his life around and maybe would he like to bring a toothbrush and a change of underwear over with him the next time he came?

He looked at her. And that's when he said that he wasn't sure but thought maybe they should take a break. Stop seeing each other for a while.

"I'm not asking you to get married! You think I'd want to marry a loser fool like you?"

He looked at her. She told him to get up.

She told him he was leaving and that he'd have to walk home because she wasn't driving him back this time or ever, nor would she give him the thirty-seven dollars he'd need for a cab, and no, she would not pack up some of the jalfrezi to take with him.

That was it.

He walked home. He sulked for a week.

His mother asked him what was wrong. A month later, she asked him if he was ready to look for job.

A month after that, she told him to leave. He asked if he could use her phone and called his old college roommate, a kind of dweeby, successful transactional analysis therapist, who took him in on the one condition that he join one of his therapy groups.

Marvin had no other choice. He got a haircut. He polished his shoes, ironed his jeans, and decided that he wanted people to call him Marlon instead of Marvin.

Marlon helped out. He did the dishes. He made dinners and coffee in the morning. They talked.

"Listen, Marlon," Seymore said, "you are only a loser fool if you choose to act like one."

He convinced Fishman that changing his name, as important as it was, was only a first step and that he needed "to change his life script."

"Marvin," he said, "was a loser because that is how he saw himself and how he let others see him. But Marlon," he said, "gets to start all over. Write a new story."

Fishman, of course, wanted a new start, but deep down he knew there was loser-ness in him. If therapy could erase that, make him a new man, then bring it on.

He wanted to believe that the others around the therapy circle were men just like him. They had to be. Why else would they be here? Why else would they subject themselves to this ridiculous self-introspection? Hoping for a magical get-out-of-loser-jail card at $150 a session?

This aside, he listened. He watched. He attended one meeting after another. It was not easy. The mere mention of what Seymore called Marlon's own parent ego state sent him into a discomfiting fog: the conflicting soft, nurturing parent part of him set against the cold, critical one within him almost manifested physically in the room, elbowing each other and tugging at his limbs.

"Marlon?"

It was Seymore.

"Marlon, can you tell us what you're thinking?"

"What?"

"You haven't said anything yet. I think we can all see that things are going on in your head."

"My mother."

"Tell us."

"My mother always told me that one day I would blame her."

"Blame her?"

"She said, 'It's always the mother. And mark my words, one day you will say that I did it to you.'"

"Did what to you?"

"I don't know."

"What do you think?"

"That one day when I'd get unhappy enough—marry the wrong person or get fired or start drinking—I'd go see a therapist, like now, and I would blame her."

"Do you?"

"I did."

"What do you mean?"

He wasn't thinking anymore. He was talking like a fisherman dragging up lines from the muck along with stringy, green weeds.

"I saw her as a weakling. She took everything my father doled out, how he treated her and made her feel like a fool, and all she'd do was get weepy."

"And?"

"And, I guess, I blamed her."

"You blamed her for...?"

"For all of that. For being weak. For my being an angry shithead. For my saying crappy insensitive things to people, treating them like shit. Not loving them."

"Marlon? Was she like that? You think she made you like that?"

Marlon looked at the men around the circle. Their faces. The way they shifted in their seats, uncrossed their legs, leaned toward him. Spilling cold coffee from their cups. He saw among them the face of his mother waiting for his answer.

"No," he said. "She loved me. She was the fragile and fearful one. Afraid of what others might think, worried about how she would survive if my father ever left her. He was the angry one. Not her."

"And?"

"And I...I think I was...was afraid of him too, but then I treated her just like he did."

"And did your father love you and treat you well?"

"No. He treated me the same way."

And then, as if by some practiced, silent signal, the men rose as one, arms outstretched, and surrounded him in a warm enveloping hug as he stood to meet them, his head bowed like a penitent.

He was no fool, he thought. Self-revelation aside, he could definitely learn to play this game.

The Pompitous of Love

I am in the backyard raking leaves and bagging them in the paper sacks we get at the hardware store. The same store I worked at in summers during college, selling socket wrenches, tenpenny nails, and ball-peen hammers.

I'm raking the leaves with Ezra. My son. He's home from school in DC for the winter break. In two weeks, his girlfriend will come visit, and then they'll drive back to school. I like her. I'm happy for him. He's crazy about her. When she's here, it seems like she never leaves his side.

It's been raining off and on for the last few weeks, and the leaves are heavy and matted, dark and pressed flat against the ground and when we rake them up, the grass underneath is soft and a tender green. Not dried up and thin with the dead color of whitherd cornstalks on the exposed parts of the yard.

"Why's the grass is so green under there?" Ezra says.

"I don't know. Maybe because it's warmer under the leaves and dark and the grass grows and greens up a little like it does when it sprouts up in the spring," I say.

"So why do we rake the leaves off it?"

"What do you mean?"

"Why don't we just leave it covered up like that all winter? Like if we weren't around? And then we could rake it up in the spring?"

I like the way he thinks. The way he makes me think. I like the things his mind holds up and turns around.

145

I don't say anything. I'd never thought about it that way.

He is looking down at the grass by his feet. "So why do you do it? What's it good for?"

"You mean is it good for the grass?"

"Yes," he says. "Or is it aesthetics? Or because everyone else does it?" His voice has deepened over the past year. He speaks more slowly than he did just the year before.

I look around. The Goodenoughs have had their lawn raked and blown clean twice already. Before any of us have brought our softening pumpkins to the transfer station.

"Aesthetics, I guess."

We hear a car and turn our heads to follow the sound.

When he sees his mother pull into the driveway, his eyes widen and a small curve comes to the corners of his lips. His cheeks round. *He's such a beautiful boy*, I think.

He loves his mother. He loves her differently from the way I do. *What is it about love? Really. How different it can be and yet still the same?*

He loved his mother the moment he took his first breath. As he was laid against her tired chest, feeling the rise and fall of her breathing. Feeling the first touch of her skin. Its familiar smell will be with him until his last day. A touchstone to his own existence.

Between them there is a kind of calibration of love that occurred in that first instant. Maybe even before that. A setting or resetting of their biological set points. Their first shared recognition of an unshakable, wordless, eternal bond.

I love her too. Perhaps in many of the same ways he does. And then in other, different, ways. Ways he will know too, but with someone else. Maybe someone who smiles like she does. Or not. But there will be something in her smile.

For me, though, it was a slower path to love her. Slow and constant. Like gravity, almost.

A willing, steady, recalibration of love for each of us. A resetting of the parameters and meaning of love.

Narrowing the distance between us, until being next to her was the only place I wanted to be. Sharing a border, like two states, for which the only thing that separates them is an invisible understanding that they are separate but inseparable.

Not enough is said about how two people come to love one another. To care for the other more than for oneself. To come to reach out in sleep for each other in the dark. To watch the other person as they grow and change. To ache when they ache.

Why do we need to know the biochemistry of love? What good would it do if we did? What can naming the neural pathways in the cingulate gyrus or the oxytocin receptors or dopamine titers in synaptic junctions can tell us about love that we don't already know or need to know?

The three of us walk back toward the house. My fingers are numbed from the cold and wet. Ezra walks ahead with his mother. I bring the rakes up to the back door. I think I'll let the leaves stay where they have fallen until they are dried up and blown away by the warming breezes we get here in late March. We'll see how that goes.

There is a picture of her I keep on my desk. In this one, we are side by side. I'm smiling, and my head is down. I'm wearing my black suit, and she's in her white dress. My hair is not yet gray, and hers is light. A few strands of it have blown across her forehead, covering her cheek. She's walking beside me, looking at me as she does so often now and her eyes are as bright and clear as the July-blue sky behind her.

The End of the Story

A few days before Christmas, a poet friend from back east, Bernard Millanowski, calls me and asks to meet for a drink. Says he's been traveling around for a while and is in Frisco for a couple days. He needs a place to stay. Sure, I say.

We meet. Dark circles around his eyes. Worry lines. Says he hasn't slept in a month. He's being followed.

It seems that back in June, he gets this call from an old ex. Her daughter, a clean-cut type, graduated from high school and broke up with her not-too-quick hockey player boyfriend on the very same day. She was going to college and he wasn't. It was fun, but yeah, end of story.

Not so, though, according to her Gordie Howe type guy, who clearly does not like the taste of that doughnut. So he takes to cruising by their house at night for weeks, leaving "see me or else" messages on the girl's phone.

They call the cops. Nothing they can do.

The mom now has to deal with the hockey puck's anger management issues. He has all the impulse control of a flannel shirt. The kid calls her and threatens her with what he'll do to her if the girl doesn't come back to him.

Next thing, he breaks into the house while she's at work, trashes the girl's room, smashes the family picture over the piano, and leaves a note on her pillow: "First installment."

So here is where Millanowski comes in. The mother calls him and says the cops came, looked around, wrote notes on their pads and said there was no proof the kid did it but they'll have a talk with him.

Bad idea. The kid gets pissed that the mom put the cops onto him, and now he threatens to get the grandma too. That afternoon, he hurls a rake through the grandma's kitchen window, knocking her potted geraniums into the sink.

So now the mom calls my friend at 2:00 a.m. She's with the grandma, and the kid just drove over their lawn. When my friend shows up, the mom hands him a loaded twenty-two. Where and how she got it, he has no idea.

Now he's playing Davy Crockett by the living room window until dawn. The kid doesn't show. He has no idea what he would have done if he had.

So one thing leads to another, and now the mom calls my friend again and says it's time to put an end to all of this. She has a plan, and she needs his help.

All he has to do is call the kid, tell him he's the family lawyer and they're ready to make a deal. No more threats. No more cops, and he'll get twenty-five grand in small bills in a plain envelope to do with whatever he wants. He just has to leave the family alone.

The mom's plan is that when the kid and my friend meet, just the two of them, by the garbage shed out behind the high school, my friend is to hand over the cash and, while the kid is counting it, the mom, who has been hiding under a pile of discarded fish sticks boxes and Captain Morgan empties, jumps out, shoves a chloroform-soaked rag in the kid's face, and jabs him in the neck with a syringe she filled with Nembutal. Where she'd get the Nembutal, he has no idea. Then they load the kid into a heavy-duty trash bag and roll him down the hill into the Kensico Reservoir, not to be seen again. End of story.

I must digress here for a moment. My friend is no thug. He's a good, hardworking, reasonable guy, a schlub of sorts, but no one remotely capable of doing this. So much for what I think I know, because he agrees to the plan.

The evening of the meet-up arrives. Midnight comes and the kid doesn't show. They leave.

The next morning, my friend is at the mom's house finishing coffee and crullers when there's a knock at the door. "Holy shit!" They have visions of the guy from *Halloween II*. My friend peeks out the window.

It's two cops.

Now my friend thinks they'll be arrested for conspiracy to commit and he's thinking he'll be spending the next fifty years doing time in Dannemora.

The cops knock again.

The mom opens the door.

"Ma'am." The cop's kind of looking past her into the living room. "We think we got your guy," he says.

They picked up the kid near the high school around ten the night before. They had been keeping an eye on him like she wanted them to. And they find a bag of weed and a Smith & Wesson shorty in his car. The kid's now being held without bail on a couple of warrants and probably won't be seen around town for a good long while.

End of story you think. No.

"And, oh," the cop says as he's leaving, "you haven't spoken to him lately, have you?"

"Me? No," she says.

The cop comes back with, "By the way, any chance you know a guy by the name of Bernard Millanowski, a lawyer? The kid said this Millanowski fellow is his dealer, and that maybe it was Millanowski who was trashing the family premises and trying to pin it on the kid."

Bernie, who is hiding behind the clothes dryer in the basement, hears his name, and it's like he all of a sudden remembers he's got to catch this train to Peoria, and he is out the back door. No forwarding address.

So I say, "End of story?"

He looks at me and his face screws up like he just licked a grapefruit. "No," he says. "The kid fingered me for pushing him the dope and selling him the gun. Which is total bullshit, but..."

I look at Bernie. I look at myself in the mirror behind the bar.

I lay a twenty on the bar, cover it with my Rolling Rock empty, pick up my keys, and make my way to the door. There is no way I'm getting involved in any of this, old friend or not.

End of story.

Alice in Chains

Alice Gompert and Harran Schlamm had once dated. Back in high school. When they both shared the crystalline innocence of a pair of snowflakes falling toward the windshield of a slow-moving Winnebago heading north on I-290.

Harran turned to her now, at age twenty-four, with his still-undiminished snowflake eyes, sitting in 'their' booth, the one they once sat in back in the old days at Marvin's Merry Melodies, an ice cream and candy shop in Evanston, Illinois. The shop, formerly a record and tape store owned by Fred Gompert, Alice's father, who presciently, on the cusp of the digital music revolution, sold off all of the stock, gutted the place, and with advice from Bob Bigelow, his brother-in-law, a self-made, wealthy entrepreneur, who said that the future of retail was in ice cream, and who set Fred up using his controlling interest in Kelley Country Creamery, the foremost ice cream maker in the state of Wisconsin, where "they know their ice cream," and he signed a ten-year exclusive Evanston sole-distributor contract with KCC, and installed vintage booths, counters, freezers, and lighting, and never found the need to change the name on the store marque.

Harran, with tentative, downcast eyes and his hand gently resting on Alice's elbow, said, "Can I ask you a question?"

She glanced at the hand on her elbow. "Yeah, sure," she said, "like what?"

They had once dated for all of four, non-consecutive, weeks. They'd been sweethearts. Or, I should say, Harran considered them as such, while from Alice's point of view, they were just friends, thoroughly devoid of any possible deeper feelings and any attendant benefits. He'd taken her to three Alice in Chains concerts, one per year, when the band played up in Kenosha. It was not the actual Alice in Chains they saw. The band was called Alice's Chains, an AIC cover band which Harran said were way better than AIC anyway. But that didn't matter. It was only the name of the band that was way cool since it included Alice's name.

Alice's parents, Fred and Lillian, had driven them, waited in the parking lot, and drove them back for ice cream at the store, opened especially just for them. Three evenings. Each of which Harran counted as a full week of dating. Then there was the senior prom to which Harran invited her the day after the night of the junior prom to which Alice had gone with George Blechta, a twitchy dweeb who danced like Elaine Benes doing a version of the Stroll. And she, of course, said yes, but ended up not going because she had a tonsillectomy the day before the prom and then spent the next six days recovering from surgery. He brought her the corsage he had purchased and counted that as week four.

He looked at her there, once again sitting together in 'their booth,' and said, "Alice, would you..."

"Harran, don't."

"Don't what?"

"Don't ask me what I think you're going to ask me."

"What do you think I..."

"Harran. I'm sorry. This is just not such a good time for me, okay?"

"Okay... Would you...," he said then, "...would you ever think of going back to New York?"

She sighed, "I don't know," and she shifted in her seat so that his hand dropped away from the warm bend of her elbow.

"I don't know," she said. "I went there because I couldn't live here anymore. This store. Opening at ten and closing at six every day, every day, and dinners at home with parsley, a starch, and a protein on every plate. This little place with its little routines and its niceties that feel like crustless white bread triangles with low fat cream cheese spread and seedless cucumber slices."

Harran looked at her as though he was listening to her.

"I went to New York to get away and I loved it. Loved every minute of it. People from all over the world in one place. Working and reading actual books. Staying up after nine o'clock and going to Czechoslovakian movies. Eating dinner at ten. People on the subways. I once sat across from Sarah Jessica Parker on the F train and it was like "oh, okay," and bumped into John Turturro in Bruno's deli in Park Slope. And when I heard Sinatra singing 'If you can make it here you can make it anywhere' on New Year's and I cried each year because it's true. True, true, true!"

"So, you're going back, then?"

"And then it all came down. It all came down around me. The buildings. The thundering, shaking noise that has never stopped in my ears. And the horrible, horrible clouds of oily, burning, grey-black smoke, choking your lungs and burning your eyes, and filling your body with such enormous fear like someone was holding onto you and who won't let you go, and you panic and plead, and they still won't let you go.

"I couldn't stay there. I tried. I tried to be normal. To feel normal. I tried. And walking in Penn Station each day with soldiers in camo, desert camo in Penn station, with machine guns pointed to the floor, their fingers so, so near the triggers. Everywhere. Street corners. And you want to cry out to make it all stop and to go back to the way it was before. But it never will. People just stopping on the street. Just stopping and putting their heads down and covering their eyes and crying. Crying so softly, hiding their faces from you. And you, you just walk by and then you start crying yourself.

You knew. You knew that all those faces, the flyers taped to the walls and the fences and light posts. They were never coming back. They were dead. You knew it because it was a nightmare in a clear blue sky. And it was the realest thing you will ever see, and never forget.

"I am covered with it all. The incinerated flesh and plastic and metal. The incinerated lives. And that morning, that same morning. On the train. At seven fifty-five. People I was sitting with, looking at their phones, holding onto the railings. At the station under the buildings. They got off and took the elevators up to work in those buildings."

"I'm sorry."

"Harran, I am not who I was before. I don't know who I am now. It's not just that the buildings fell. It's how and why it happened. The senselessness of it. How people planned this murder. And others knew about it and said, 'yes, go do it.' And governments knew, had to have known, and were complicit. For what? To make us feel attacked and attackable. Vulnerable. Ultimately, personally, vulnerable. Not theoretically. Not philosophically. But materially, demonstrably, vulnerable."

"I'm sorry."

"I know you are. And I know you cannot know what I'm feeling. The feeling that you matter less than nothing. And that nothing matters. Realizing that everything matters. That everything matters so little and yet that everything matters so much. That breathing and trees matter. The sky, the person sitting next to you, the woman in the library or the one working the fryolator in McDonald's. They all matter. That everything matters and nothing matters.

"And then what? Instead of sadness, healing, and introspection, Hillary fucking Clinton and Chuck fucking Schumer voted, voted in the Senate, to knowingly, calculatingly, bomb and burn and incinerate thousands more people? To plan it. Execute it. Calling it 'shock and awe' like a Call of Duty video game. I knew better. They knew better. And still they voted to say go ahead to George fucking W. Bush and his fucking father who was once the director of the CI fucking A. He knew about the Saudis. They all knew about it. They could have stopped it all and they just went ahead and did it with smiles on their faces."

"Please don't say that."

"Say what?"

"Fucking."

"Oh my God, Harran. Me saying 'fucking'? That's what bothers you? I shouldn't say fucking in my father's fucking candy store, in Evanston fucking Illinois? Because it may disturb some people? They should be fucking disturbed. Take a look around, Harran, has anyone one died because they heard me say ''fucking?'''

"Alice."

"Don't tell me Alice. I'm not Alice. I don't know who this person is anymore. I'm going."

"Don't go. Where are you going?"

"I don't fucking know, Harran. You know that feeling of waking up in the middle of the night because you feel like you're falling? That's the feeling I have every night. But *I* wake up in the morning and they don't. Can you imagine the feeling of falling, to be falling, to have the room falling with you, the ceiling crushing down on you, as the last feeling you will ever have in life? I pray you don't ever know what that feels like. I have to go."

"Why did you even come back?"

"What?"

"Why did you come back?"

"Don't ask me that. I don't know. I think I was hoping things would be different here. But they're not. I'm not."

"Could you let me out?" he said.

"What?"

"Let me out. I have to go."

The Cat, the Crease, and the Cosmos

Gunther looks as pale as a piece of pickled herring. Lines and wires stick in him like he's a trussed-up boiled chicken.

"I feel like shit," he tells me.

"Everybody in here must feel like shit," I say.

"Did I tell you?" he says. "When the nurse was prepping me for surgery, she said to me, 'You know, you're pretty lucky. You got that crease in your earlobe.' So I say to her, 'And...?' And she says to me, 'And...most people with an earlobe crease like that show up a little too late, and downstairs they go with a yellow tag on their toe.' No joke. She said that."

So I say to him, "She tells you this while you're lying there with angina like an anvil and one MI already in the can, and who knows what else is coming next? For what? To boost your spirits?"

"Exactly. So I ask Claire to find out what she's talking about, but they wheel me out before she gets back. And next thing, when I wake up, Claire says, 'How's the crease today?' like I wasn't already dreaming of dancing earlobe creases with brooms carrying the buckets of water like in that old Disney cartoon where Mickey Mouse is wearing the sorcerer's hat."

I tell him I have absolutely no clue as to what he's talking about. "What crease in what sorcerer's hat?"

And he tells me that some study found that an earlobe crease like his is a sign of a coronary waiting to happen, as if this was some well-known scientific fact.

And I say, "If it's so well-known, why'd they wait to tell you this when you're lying on a table like a meatloaf with a white sheet covering your cold and clammy behind?"

Needless to say, neither of us can answer that one. But then he starts talking about the universe and how he thinks maybe there is more going on than we think there is, and that when he was in the ICU he started thinking about spirituality and the universe and quarks and things I never ever heard him say before.

Of course, I think he's just not getting enough blood flow to his brain, and that's when he says, "All of a sudden it hit me, like I was walking down a flight of stairs and thinking I had one more step and I put my foot down and there's no more step and the adrenaline lights up every nerve circuit in my body, and stuff I never thought about before starts making sense, like my mind is opening up and filling the entire room and flowing out the window. I mean, you know me," he says, "I am totally deity-free. I don't believe in much of anything, like when my cousin Elaine says she was once an Egyptian princess or a bus driver in Poughkeepsie or whatever. But then I think that maybe there is some stuff out there, like gravity or electromagnetism were before they figured them out, and maybe we can't see it or feel it until somebody gives it a name."

"Like?"

"Like, you ever hear of Heisenberg's uncertainty principle? Or Schrödinger's cat? No, I didn't think so. But let me tell you, it all makes sense to me. Like a weird kind of spiritual reality. Those electrons and positrons or muons or whatever from way back in the beginning of everything are the same ones in you and me and everything else, but we can't see them or know where they're going because they could be a wave or a particle or both at the same time and they could be in one part of the universe or in another. And I mean the same one, at exactly the same time, could be here and there and in both places at the same time, but we can only see it in one of them because that's the place we're looking."

I don't know much, but I do know that doesn't make sense. Newton, I think I understand. "And what's with the cat?" I say.

"Yeah, the cat! So this guy Schrödinger thinks, what if you seal a cat in a box with a radioactive device that may or may not go off within an hour, and it either kills the cat or doesn't. So there's this 50 percent chance the cat is alive and a 50 percent chance it's dead. Right? The cat logically exists in two different, equally probable states at one time with a 100 percent probability of it being alive and dead in the instant before you open the box. But when you open the box, it is only in one and you never get to see the cat when it's in both."

And now I'm thinking, like *you* must be, *I'll have what he's having.* But he's clearly not finished.

"Well," he says, "here's where it gets 'do-do-do-do' spiritual. Not only can electrons simultaneously be in two different places at the same time, like in my fingernail and in a moon rock in Alpha Centauri, but if something changes the spin of the one in my fingernail, then its twin, the one in Alpha Centauri, instantaneously, by some mysterious entanglement, 25.7 trillion miles away, changes in exactly the same way. Boom! Can you possibly explain that?"

Obviously, I can't. I say, "You mean all the electrons or bozotrons or whatever in the whole universe are entangled, like you say, with one another. And we, you and me, are connected to every other particle in the whole universe?"

"That's it. That is totally it," he says. "How much more beyond 'because the Bible tells me so' can anything be? How much more spiritual can anything be? C'mon, man, you get it, don't you? Something that is so elemental that it existed in the nothing at the beginning of everything is still here now, right? You're damn right we're all connected, all made from the very same bits of electrons, photons, leptons, muons, and morons."

"Morons?"

"Never mind," he says.

I'm ready to go, but just to be sure, I say, "And this has *what*, exactly, to do with the nurse and your earlobe crease?"

"Who knows?" he says. "All I know is I love you, man!"

There's a good chance he won't remember a single word of any of this tomorrow.

Thinking Now of Your
White-Whiskered Dog and Other Things

Your white-whiskered dog sits by you when you read. She lies under the table at your feet when you eat. She follows you around the house. She knows where you are going when you leave the house and when you'll be back just by the shoes you put on.

Her fourteen-year-old brown eyes are clouded now. Her soft-waved black Scotty hair and random patches of gray. Much like yours was back when you first saw her. Back when your children, like all children, said, "Yes, yes, we promise we'll feed her and walk her every day."

And then the woman who owned the dog unfastened her collar as she strained against the tie-out line she was on in the woman's backyard and she hopped, in one leap, onto the back seat of your car and you brought her home. And she slept that night in the bed you bought from the pet store in town, on the floor in your room, beside your bed.

She came to you with red and blue chew toys that she never played with and the tie-out line you don't use. You never could get the green, battery-powered bark-stop collar to work, but all you needed to do to stop her insistent barking at the window was hold it up and show it to her and she would crouch down on the back of the sofa by the window with her head low, and the loud barking would stop and you felt good and bad about that at the same time.

And now you know that when she pees on the rug in the spare room where you keep your books stacked on the floor, that she can't help it because she has a tumor growing in her bladder, but you also think that maybe she is upset with you, in her way, because you have taken in a homeless, abandoned kitten.

The kitten is black too. She has mites and allergies, and she's tiny. No bigger than a rolled-up ball of wool socks, with big yellow eyes and silky fur that has a brown tint in it when the sun angles on it and when she stretches out her white paws to you so that you'll rub her chin and smooth her white belly. And when you do, she reaches out and holds onto your hand with her front paws and her sharp, gentle teeth and pinwheels her back paws fast against your hand with her pink baby-skin pads. Just like she did the first time she got out of the house and caught the pale brown and gray spotted house sparrow she chased down like a jaguar in the neighbor's yard and lay down next to it until you found her. When you picked up the young bird from where she had dropped it in the rough dirt, you could feel its weightless dying in your palm and see your reflection in its dull eyes, now matte and black while, only a moment ago, they had been lucent and bright.

You think of how fleeting it all is and how quickly everything seems to pass.

Your old dog with the tumor growing in her belly follows you from room to room, with just the smallest pink tip of her tongue protruding from her mouth, as you clean the blinds and sweep the floor and make the coffee. How she waits for you, lying stretched out on her side outside of the bathroom door so you can bend over and pat her on the back of her head, where you can feel the hard, round growths there now that were only modest bumps months ago and which the vet said we would need to keep an eye on.

Still, each day, she eagerly walks with you on the horse path along the stream, where the beavers cut down the young white birch trees and drag them down into the water. She lags behind, sniffing at their pointed stumps, and then sprints as she always has done when she sees you with your arms spread out wide, as if saying "Where've you been?" and you both hike up a ways into the woods and around the lake.

And now you stand at the kitchen sink with your second cup of coffee, and the little cat jumps up on the counter to look out the window. Your old dog sits on her aching haunches and pads her front paws up and down, waiting for you, looking up at you, clicking her nails in anticipation, which also gets your attention, so you'll remember to give her a piece of the whole wheat toast you made, warm with butter and red raspberry jam. You forgot you were holding it while you were looking out the window above the kitchen sink and watching the stiff old birch tree sway and creak in the frozen wind. You were thinking of other things. Of how fleeting it all is, and how dear is the hope for peace at the end.

Adelaide on the Beach

When Sedge saw the body on the beach in the evening, he didn't believe, didn't want to believe, that it was Adelaide, the woman he had been seeing for a few months until they had wordlessly drifted away from each other. They had never, he thought, made any sort of commitment to each other, save for the general assumption that they'd spend an evening or two together, sometimes during the week when she was in town, but mostly on the weekends, starting at one of the bars along the A1A strip up by Fort Pierce and having a few drinks and maybe sharing a plate of peel-and-eat shrimp or maybe the conch fritters, which she liked better, even though they were greasy and she'd have to take a Zantac if she remembered to bring them with her, and also because she didn't like how the smell of the shrimp on her fingers would linger for hours and keep her from letting her tease herself with the smell of Sedge on her after he left. Usually, he left some hours before sunrise but after the sky had lightened over the water in the east, which she could see from the windows in the condo she rented, but before the beach-goers had set up their chairs and umbrellas—with the exception, of course, of the brown-skinned men in wide Panama hats and long-sleeved shirts who dug their tall fishing rods into the sand and tried to catch the blues or whatever was running from the tuna that early in the day.

Sedge felt a shudder run down his spine, down into his legs, behind his knees, from the flush of adrenaline or whatever chemical it is that plunges into your veins and courses through your blood and heart and lungs and stomach even before your eyes have adjusted to what you are seeing. Like the way the screech of tires somehow makes you feel before you even actually hear them in your brain or feel the crush of the metal all around you, throwing you into the exploding airbags and breaking your fall and your nose.

And by then he was sure that it *was* her, with men and a few women standing around her with their big towels around their waists and their heads bent to her. She was lying on her stomach on the sand with her arms spread out away from her, limp and wide, and her head turned away to the other side as if she could not bear to think of him looking at her lying flat on the beach in the black bathing suit she loved and thought she looked stunning in and how he might think that she'd worn the same bathing suit two days in a row instead of washing it in the evening and hanging it to dry on the railing of the deck of the condo, soaking up the morning sun and the freshness of the sea. And could not bear for him to see her hair, red and clogged with clumps of sand and bits of seaweed, and the grains of sand adhering to her back and her thighs in a way that would make her feel dissolute and unladylike. And as if she wanted him to look away from her and walk back up the beach while the other men and women stood over her in a rough circle like huge, mournful Neolithic Stonehenge sarsen sandstone pillars, blocking the sun and creating long shadows across her body, with one of them pointing toward her with a beach towel as if questioning whether or not they should cover her before the police came and talking in soft tones as if to spare her from hearing the criticism in their funereal voices that perhaps only she, if she were alive, could sense, in the way she always had.

Just like her father had done in the years before he left her, her mother, and her sister in the one-bedroom apartment in Kissimmee, where she had slept on the pullout couch and had been expected, even at the age of seven, to wash and dress herself and make her own breakfast and fold the bed back up into the rank and moldy innards of the couch. Where she heard, on the first day of every month, the rapping on the door as she picked up the trash and bottles from the kitchen floor and put them in the bin as she had been told to do when the landlord came for the rent, peeking in over her shoulder, breathing his foul breath and touching her on the small of her back in a way that chilled her and made gooseflesh on her arms. She would tell him that he should come back in the evening to see her father, who had the money for him, while her father, at that very moment, was lying in his shorts and T-shirt with his arm across her mother before she dressed and left for work at the nail salon in Orlando six days a week, knowing that the life she had was not the life she wanted nor wanted for her daughter Adelaide.

And her mother prayed that when Adelaide was old enough, she would leave this place with its guns and ammo shops and massage parlors and have a life that would bring her a little happiness, a little rest, and a man who would treat her right, treat her like a woman wants to be treated. She told Adelaide that that life would come to her because she was smart and strong and wily, to which Adelaide would laugh and tell her mother that she never wanted to be like Wile E. Coyote because he's the one who always runs off the edge of the cliff or has an anvil falling down on him and maybe he dies or maybe he doesn't, but she didn't really know because she'd always put her hands over her eyes and turn away from the TV when she saw that starting to happen, and she hoped that it would never, ever, happen to her.

And then her mother would grab her up in her soft, white arms and hold her as tight as could be. She would squeeze Adelaide's breath out of her and say, "Adelaide, my baby, that will never happen to you," and when Sedge saw her lying there in her black bathing suit in the center of the growing crowd on the sand with the tide receding, his heart sank into his knees. He sat down right there where he had been standing, and he put his hands over his eyes so that he would not see what would happen next.

The Double

Yakov awakens in a hospital bed. He does not remember being brought here. He does not recall a fall or feeling ill. He has simply found himself in a hospital bed, wearing a cotton gown tied loosely behind him and an ID band secured around his wrist. On it is his birth date and his name: Schecter, Yakov P. *What on earth?* he wonders. *What is this? What has happened to me?*

His glasses are on the tray table in front of him. His folded newspaper. His cell phone. A card to him from his co-workers at the firm. "Get well soon." A menu with his choices circled for lunch and dinner. He is sharing the room with another person.

He lifts the cover off the plate in front of him. A few crumbs of a muffin and a cup of uneaten applesauce. He remembers eating nothing.

The man in the other bed, the one with a view by the window, is speaking on the phone. The man's voice sounds familiar to Yakov, but it's not one he can place with any certainty.

Someone knocks on the door to the room. "Mr. Schecter?" she calls out. A nurse in a blue smock. She pulls on a pair of exam gloves, and before Yakov can answer, the man with a congenial-sounding voice in the bed by the window calls back to her, "Yes, come in."

Yakov looks at the whiteboard on the wall in front of him. His own name is right there: Yakov Schecter, in black marker. Becky, it says, is his nurse. *This must be Becky*, he thinks. The doctor's name is Rutenberg, not a name he recognizes.

"Don't you mean me?" Yakov says to her.

"Oh no, not you. I mean Mr. Schecter, over there."

Yakov sits on the edge of his bed. He leans over and pulls the curtain away until he can see the other man. He is old. Older looking than his voice suggested. Maybe in his late eighties. Jowly. His right leg is amputated at the knee. His hair is close-cropped. He is unshaven. The bones of his shoulders protrude like those of an old, withered cow. *Have I seen this face before?* Yakov thinks to himself.

The nurse props a pillow behind the other man's head. Asks him if he needs anything, inquires about his family, and adjusts the shades on the window.

After the nurse leaves, Yakov pulls the curtain over a little more so they can look at each other. "My name's Schecter, Yakov," he says.

"Pleased to meet you, Mr. Schecter. I'm a Schecter too. Also a Yakov," the man tells him. "We could be related. Wouldn't that be something!"

"You must be kidding."

"Well," is all the man says.

"You know, you look a lot like…" says Yakov.

At that, the nurse returns with a cup of juice. "Mr. Schecter, I have the juice you asked for."

She places it on the old man's tray.

"Bring me one too," says Yakov.

"I'm not your nurse. You will have to ask your nurse," she tells him.

"That was uncalled for. All I asked for was some juice. You don't have to be so—"

"Listen to me, Yakov," says the old man. "I've been watching you. You treat them right, like I do, and they'll treat you right."

Yakov does not know what to think. *I have treated no one badly. Not complained once until just this minute.* He cannot remember saying anything unkind to the nurse. All he did was to tell the nurse to bring him a glass of juice. *After all, that's what they pay them for.*

"I will try," he says.

"You should. You know people pick up vibes. Not me, mind you, but people."

Yakov pulls the curtain closed. *This is insane,* he thinks. He picks up the newspaper and rings for his nurse.

He waits. No response. He rings again.

"Is this your doing, Schecter?" he says to the man on the other side of the curtain. "What have you said to them about me? What have you got against me? I thought we might be friends."

"I am your friend," says Mr. Schecter. "I care about you. And that's some wheeze you've got there, Yakov. You should have it looked at."

"What do you mean, I should get it looked at? Who are you to tell me what I should do? That's *your* wheeze you hear, anyway, not mine. I shouldn't even be here. There is nothing wrong with me."

"No? Maybe, maybe not. But perhaps it is your attitude. I know men like you. I know them quite well. Men who think they're better than others. Men who would step on you if it would help them in some way, even if it was only in their own mind."

Yakov has had just about all he can take from this guy, and the nurse, and everyone out in the hall, who he knows are talking about him.

"You know," he says, talking to the curtain, "let me tell *you* something. Now I know you're nuts and you, for some unknown reason, are just trying to piss me off. Make me think I'm crazy or something. You're the one with the wheeze. You're the one with the bum leg and the bedsores as big as meatballs. That's you. Not me. You're on your last trip to the grocery store here, man, not me. I have a job. I'm a law clerk. I know my rights. I have a life. I have responsibilities you'll never have. I'm getting out of here. I'm not you."

"Maybe, maybe not."

The next morning, Yakov Schecter awakens in a hospital bed in a double room. From his bed by the window, he has a clear view of the sailboats tacking and turning on the silver-blue river.

What a relief! That old man with the bum leg and the wheeze who calls himself Yakov Schecter, the imposter, is gone! Perhaps he died and they took his body away during the night. But yet, he thinks, *I don't recall being moved, and shouldn't I be the one leaving? Going home. To work. There is nothing wrong with me. I am healthy. I am young. I have an important job I need to get to. A terrible mistake has been made.*

And there is rustling behind the curtain. He hears a man in the bed on the other side of the curtain. He can hear the man coughing. Calling for the nurse to come in.

He hears the nurse come in. A rustling sound. She is on the other side of the curtain.

Perhaps, as he has heard in whispering at the office and occasionally among others in his loose social circle, that he is arrogant. Yes. And overbearing. Officious. Yes, of course when it is necessary. And superstitious. No. What could they mean. He is a believer in the real and the observable. *I see things as they are,* he thinks. *That is why this whole situation is so disturbing. Am I mad? How is one to know?*

There is another rustling of the curtains. If she is coming his way, he will certainly do his best to be considerate and polite.

"Mr. Schecter?" the nurse says.

The Girl with the Ruby-Red Lips

You're going to forget people. You think you never will. But trust me, you will. You'll lose track of them and then you'll forget them. Their names and faces will disappear. You'll forget things too, like how many ounces are in a pound of cottage cheese or if you've had breakfast. But you think it won't happen...

And then you'll grow up and go to college and meet someone and maybe have kids and you'll go hiking in the Adirondacks, and your parents will die, and then suddenly you'll find yourself sitting in a wheelchair at a table in a blue-painted room with palm trees stenciled on the wall. You'll be sitting with three other people you don't recognize who are wearing dark sunglasses inside, and there are posters in the halls with "Today's Date Is" on them and the names of everyone with a birthday that week, and a woman with a voice like a soft sweet song puts a plate of baked salmon with parslied potatoes and three sweet gherkins down in front of you and tells you to "eat it all up jus' like a good bwoy."

And then you'll think of things, of lost people, just like how the aroma of those sweet gherkins makes me think of my old friend Teddy Ackerman who was not so good at geometry, but he could really play the piano. And how Mr. McGhouly would throw a piece of chalk at him and say, "Hey, piano boy, how many angles in an isosceles triangle?" And Teddy would say, "Um, isosceles?" ducking his head behind his three-ring binder.

And how after school we'd stop at Logue's Deli near the hardware store and buy a small paper tray of sweet gherkin pickles for thirty-five cents and then go to Teddy's house to study the geometry theorems and corollaries together on his back patio while his sister, Eleanor, would be sitting on the low bench at their black piano with the lid open and her back straight and her dark, dark brown hair pinned up in back with a small silver comb. Her long fingers on the keys, she wouldn't even look up when we passed by.

She was a senior that year, and she wore black skirts with nylons and white blouses with collars and white buttons in front, and everyone at school talked about how she made out with the music teacher just so he could get her into Smith College with a scholarship so she'd be a famous opera singer at the Met one day.

Teddy's house was three floors high and had a driveway that went all the way from one street to another, and his father had a big belly that hung over his belt, and he smoked cigars and took the train into the city every day.

His mother stayed at home and fretted, scoured, and economized. She told us not to make a mess with the gherkins, and she put tea towels on our laps and waited until we said, "Thank you, Mrs. Ackerman." When she opened the patio door, we could hear Eleanor playing the piano and singing, and I'd think about how red her lips were and how she made them into an O when she sang and her chin sometimes would tremble when she sang in a certain way.

And I'd imagine old Mr. Deanto making out with her standing in the band room with the music stands and chairs all around them with the lights off and how it might feel to have my hand touch her back and feel the cotton of her blouse and her warm skin and the touch of her breasts against me like two round scoops of vanilla ice cream, and how she would make her lips into an O and kiss me and how my mouth would feel with them on mine and smell her lipstick and how the muscles on my stomach would get tight and it would be hard to breathe and how my head would feel light and I would close my eyes and want to be nowhere else in the whole world but right there in the band room kissing Teddy's sister and never get caught and no one would ever know and I would remember how it felt for the rest of my life.

And before you pick one up of those gherkins or whatever and put it in your mouth, it will all come back to you, and you'll feel the glands in the way back of your mouth under your tongue squeezing like lemons, and like from out of nowhere you'll remember study-ing geometry or whatever, just like the way I remember Teddy's sister playing piano in the other room.

And then the woman with the voice like a soft sweet song will say to you, "Mr. Marty, you should eat your salmon before you eat the gherkins because the salmon is good for your brains."

And you'll say to her, "Philistine, please tell me, is there a girl here with ruby-red lips, a little older than me, by the name of Eleanor?"

And she'll tell you, "Firs', Mr. Marty, my name is Ernestine. Secon', there is no one here older than you, and third, no, there is no one here name Eleanor. And fourth, you tell me dat same question ever' time we have salmon wid gherkins for dinner. So now I tell you go and eat your salmon like I tol' you to and forget about de girl wid de ruby-red lips."

Letters from Camp Surprise Lake

On the first night at Camp Surprise Lake, Izzy Rasmussen wet his bed. A real soaker. He was in the top bunk, above Lester Himmelblatt. Lester slept soundly.

Izzy stripped the sheets off his bed and stuffed them into the bottom of his father's army-green duffel bag that his mother had sent with him on the bus from Port Authority.

She had packed three pairs of shorts, four polo shirts, underwear, and socks for three or four days, one pair of sheets, a pillowcase, three pieces of folded lined notebook paper, a pencil, three envelopes, four *Superman* comics, a toothbrush, one towel, one change of Lone Ranger pajamas, and a clean black plastic pocket comb with the name "ACE" printed on it.

He changed into dry clothes in the gray predawn light, wedged the bag in the space under Lester's bed, and sat on the front steps of the cabin.

During rest time after lunch, he wrote the following letter:

Dear Mommy and Daddy,

Camp is Great. I hope you are having a good time
with my new baby sister. Please tell her I said hello. Ha ha!
Camp is beautiful. We had egg salad with lettuce, pickles,
and Ritz crackers for dinner last night and I thought of all
the starving children in China and I finished it all.

Please send me a copy of Moby DICK. Ha ha!

Me.

Age 9

P.S. Please send me two more sheets and pajamas. I had an accident.

On Tuesday afternoon, his third day away, he scribbled the following note:

Dear Mommy and Daddy,

You did not pack any stamps for me. Was that a joke? Ha ha! Mr. Sherman said the post office wouldn't take the letter I sent you. He loaned me two stamps, which he will add to the bill. I think Neil Trushin stole my comic books, but he said that they were his and they weren't that good anyway, so he sold them.

Izzy

Age 9

P.S. We had a social with the girls' side and a girl with red hair named Fern asked me to dance. She had nice breath. I still need the sheets.

On Wednesday afternoon, he wrote the following note:

Dear Mommy and Daddy,

I made lanyards for you and grandma and stitched a fake leather wallet for daddy. Does he already have a wallet? I did not know what to make for the sister. Maybe you could buy her something. Things are not going so great here. You forgot to pack my baseball glove, and Sidney Hersh called me a homo commie dickweed and then he punched me in the shoulder.

Your son Izzy

Age 10

P.S. The red-haired girl lives in Malvern, Long Island.
Is that far away? I still need the sheets.

On Thursday afternoon, he wrote:

Dear Mommy and Daddy,

Camp is not turning out so good. Sidney took everything
out of my duffel bag. He said he thought it was his. He called
me a stinking sissy homo commie creep. I told him I liked
homo commie dickweed better and he punched me in the
other shoulder. Ask Daddy how the Dodgers are doing. Ha
ha! I think I only want to stay one week. Please come pick
me up on Sunday, not Saturday. There's another dance on
Saturday. We had egg salad again. I ate the lettuce and pickles,
but I asked them to send the egg salad to China. Fern said
they tasted like dinosaur eggs. Ha ha!

Your one and only son,

Izzy

Age 10 and 1 day

P.S. Mr. Sherman said he would not charge you for the
extra pieces of paper he loaned me, but you still owe him
for the stamps.

P.S. Sheets

On Monday afternoon, he wrote:

Dear Parents,

Do you remember me? You forgot to pick me up. I am
not feeling so well. Mr. Sherman said I should not write
to you anymore. He said he will call you. I hope you will
answer the phone. I am not kidding. Ha ha.

I found out what the surprise in the lake is. I was
swimming with Fern Dorfman today and when we got

out of the lake, Bonnie Lefrak and Sandy Klein started
screaming. The whole camp started to run away but Mr.
Sherman threw a towel around us, and then they all came
back. I am in the infirmary. I think they took all the leeches
off me. It really hurt a lot. I asked them if I could keep
one to bring home. Ha ha! Please come and pick me up
tomorrow. I really mean it.

P.S. Fern needs a ride home too. Maybe her parents
can bring me home.

P.S. Camp was not a good idea

Me

The Woman Next Door

Benson was awakened by the sounds of the woman next door leaving for work. It was seven in the morning. He didn't get out of bed.

It was cold and the rain had turned to wet snow—at least it had at 3:00 a.m. when he'd gotten up to pee. Their apartments were next to each other with only a thin gypsum-board wall between them. He knew she could hear him during the night as he fumbled for the light in the dark and then flushed the toilet. The intimacy of this embarrassed him, though there was nothing else he could do.

He and the woman talked and sometimes shared a meal together, usually in his apartment as his had a working stove, but mostly they kept to themselves.

The woman left at seven each morning. She walked up the street from the apartment, passing the railroad station and the Rite Aid and the shuttered IGA, where Benson and she had met when they both worked there, until the owners shuttered the place, letting all the people go.

When they'd shown up for work that morning, the lights were off and a sign was taped to the glass front doors among faded flyers for cat sitters, guitar lessons, and cleaning services. The sign said "Store Closed." It was printed in hasty pencil, and they had to lean up close to read it. The space has been empty now for a few years.

Now, each day, the woman walked up the hill to the horse farm to her new job. She mucked out the stalls three times a day:

once in the morning and then again around two and then in the early evening, walking back home after each shift. The horses had well-dressed owners who visited them, mostly on weekends. One horse there was called Ojai, just like the town she had grown up in.

She recited poetry while she worked. Poems by Stevens, and Bishop, and Pound, she said. Poems she had studied at Amherst... before she had the breakdown in her sophomore year and had to leave...and then was unable to return...and then had her loans to pay off and no health insurance. With meds to pay for, she had to find a job, and she couldn't find one or a place to live in Amherst in the seventies. And so she went back home to live with her parents. They didn't get along.

He didn't know how she ended up living next door.

Benson watched her leave from his window in her red Wellies, hooded wool coat, and a knit watch cap. The snow then was blowing in tight, biting drifts.

After her evening shift, the woman would stop at the library to use the bathroom and check her email and Facebook feed.

A couple had lived in the apartment next door before, where the woman lived now.

The husband was a sculptor. Short, sparsely bearded, thick-fingered. They'd invite Benson over for instant coffee and he'd fix their faucet leaks or replace burned out light bulbs in the ceiling fixtures.

One day, the wife died in the apartment. She had asthma or emphysema or something like that, coughing all of the time. That afternoon, she coughed and wheezed so hard until she stopped, and Benson heard her fall to the floor. The man—Carl was his name—tried but couldn't pick her up.

Benson heard Carl call 911. But he'd given the operator the wrong address, one they had when they lived in another city. Benson listened as he argued with the operator, screaming into the phone.

After the woman died, Benson thought he should have gone over, should have just walked in and helped, maybe should have called the police himself, but he didn't.

The snow tapered off in the evening. The temperature dropped quickly. The sky was coal black, and the woman had not yet returned. There had been a time once, she'd told him, that she had slipped on the slick black ice on the hill down from the stable. She'd broken two ribs then.

Benson pulled on a thick sweater and his hat and knocked on the woman's door. Maybe she'd come in and he hadn't heard her.

When she didn't answer, he set off up the hill, the cold tearing his eyes and catching his breath. His nose ran, freezing in the beard against his chin.

Lights were lit in the houses he passed, set back from the road, their driveways not yet plowed. He knew so few people in town. Fewer still were those who you could count on. People, he knew, had their own lives and their own troubles.

The woman next door was a good person. She liked animals, knew poetry, complained little, and had had another life, like he once did, before this one. One with a family, laughter, a backyard, and a car.

The library was closed. The woman wasn't at the gas station or sitting by the steamed-up window in the pizza shop on the corner to get warm.

He was sure he'd find her. He wouldn't go back home until he did, and then they'd walk back to the apartment together. He'd offer to heat up some dinner for them. And then they might talk about the weather and horses.

And then, when she'd go back to her place, he'd make himself a cup of tea and sit in his chair and try to read Bukowski. He'd listen to the woman washing up until his eyes would close and he'd fall asleep with a blanket pulled tightly up under his chin, until two or three when having to pee would wake him up and he'd get into bed.

When Harry Met Irene

When Harry met Irene, he was living in a state of blissful bachelor squalor. Irene as much as told him so. She was a woman of simple, straightforward, unabashed, and colorful candor.

She drove a lemon-yellow 1985 Chrysler LeBaron convertible with whitewall tires. She shaved her hair down to the nub and wore wigs. Crimson one day, indigo or persimmon the next. The wigs were set in soft ringlets that bounced when she walked.

The bounce was mostly due to the fact that her left leg was a half inch shorter than her right. She said she liked the bounce and jiggle in her step. Aside from once slipping a pair of matchbooks into the heel of her shoe, as you might do to level a table in a cheap west-side diner, she liked the way her legs worked just the way they were.

They had met by accident. He was going in the "in" door at the city services building on West 23rd Street. It was a Saturday and his day off from work at the Superb Zipper Factory on Ninth. It had previously been a button factory, which he found much easier on his fingers, but he stayed with the building when it changed hands. He had just finished a few hours of handball at the 92nd Street Y up on Lexington and was still in his sneakers and damp sweats. He was coming in to pick up hearing aid batteries. They were sixty-seven cents each, cheaper there than the ones at the Duane Reade near his apartment.

And there was Irene, coming *out* of the very same "in" door. She was blooming with the flower of self-efficacy and accomplishment, having just signed a long-term contract with her booking agent at City Sign Language Talent Consultants, LLC.

Harry backed out of the way and told her he was sorry. She looked him over and signed in his face, "Look where you're going next time, bub!" He understood not a single word.

The next time he saw her was weeks later when he was at the Y for an afternoon lecture on the enduring influence of 1940s Borscht Belt humor on post-modern stand-up comedy.

And there was Irene once again, now adorning the podium, dressed in an ochre pantsuit with a magenta scarf draped over her left shoulder. When the speaker at the lectern began talking, Irene began signing.

"So, listen," said the speaker, "have you heard the one about the old Jewish man who was rescued from drowning at Jones Beach?" He paused and looked slowly over the crowd. "Well, the lifeguard brings him in to shore, lays him down on a blanket, and says to him, 'Tell me, are you comfortable?' And the portly old man looks up at him, arches an eyebrow, and answers, 'I make a living.'"

Irene then added, in sign, her own flourish of "Ba-dump-bump!"

After the talk, Harry approached her and asked if she wanted to grab a cup of coffee. She agreed, and at Effy's Israeli Café in the basement of the Y, he ordered a coffee and a thick slice of the pineapple cheesecake. She had a tuna on rye toast with mayo, lettuce, tomato, an extra pickle, a side of herring in cream sauce, and a seltzer, no ice, with a slice of lime.

While they were eating, she said, "Harry, you're humming!"

"Beg pardon?" he replied through a mouthful of cheesecake.

"You're humming, Harry. You know you hum when you chew?"

"What's that? Honey in my stew? Never tried it."

She let it go.

Afterward, he invited her up to his third-floor prewar apartment on 96th and 1st.

He unlocked the door, reached in, and flicked on the light. The TV had been left on, he said, for the cats. Unopened mail and newspapers covered the floor. There were books in stacks like monuments to dust motes.

She peeked in. The fetid odor of his aging, matted cats; half-eaten cartons of greasy pan-fried garlic noodles; and uncountable half-pairs of unwashed gym socks and shorts hit her. He was oblivious. This was home.

"This place is a hellhole, Harry!" she told him. "I'll wait here while you clean up."

He brought a folding chair out for her to sit on, and in fifteen minutes he came back out with four chock-full thirty-three-gallon flexible black trash bags, which he forced into the garbage chute at the end of the hall. Then he turned back to her with a grin, adjusted his tie, and opened the door again.

She took a sniff and said, while signing to him, "This is much better, Harry, much, much better." She added, "But not so fast, Harry. I need some gloves, and you need a carpet sweeper."

He interpreted this as: "Butternut, at last. Harry, he's one lover, indeed an ardent keeper."

Harry looked at Irene, hearing but not quite understanding. He looked back into the apartment and back at Irene, and for the first time in all of his sixty-six years of untroubled and self-absorbed bachelordom, Harry Wiederhorn had fallen in love.

The Grocer and the Grocer's Wife

It is nearing dinnertime. Angie is making her Ligurian pesto. Two handfuls of bucatini are boiling on the stove.

"Vito," she calls out from the kitchen window.

She can hear the soft chuffing of the old manual push mower. The whir and click as he pushes it forward and pulls it back. Pushing it out, angling it to the left and then to the right, clean-cutting through the thick grass. Back and forth so that the blades of grass stand up for an even cut.

She calls again, hearing an urgency in her own voice, though at this moment she has completely forgotten what it was she wanted to tell him. Needed to tell him. Or was it something she wanted to ask him?

In his small front yard, he is conscious only of the deep-green leaves under his feet and the damp clippings falling against his scuffed black shoes. In these moments, this dark green patch and its early summer smell are all that exist in the universe.

The sleeves of his white shirt are rolled to the elbows, his collar is open, the cuffs of his faded grocer's pants are turned up. These are the pants his sister sent him from Palermo after his father passed, God rest his soul. The very pants his father wore and which Vito wears to work in the morning.

Each day, for three years now, he has driven to the Hunt's Point Market down the New York Thruway, past Yankee Stadium, to select the peaches, the broccoli, the melons, and the red and yellow peppers he arranges in rows in the canted boxes in the front of his shop, hours before the women with their Whole Foods bags awaken and walk up along 10th Avenue to heft and sniff each piece before they hand their selections to him to weigh.

A runnel of sweat slides down the hollow line of Angie's back. The kitchen is hot and steamy. Vito has not yet moved the pots and the dishes out to the cupboards in the summer kitchen in the garage. He is late this year.

Fifty-two years married. Loving him all these years. He is her man, but this place he brought her to is not her place. This place so far from her friends and family. This place of long driveways and closed curtains, locked doors, and stern faces. A place of privileged cats and tandem kayaks and children who knock on her door with raffles for round-trip tickets to Iceland.

Her heart aches to be back in their apartment on President Street, to walk on the cracked sidewalks to evening mass and to the shops on Court Street. To talk with women who look and speak like she does. She prays each night, while Vito sleeps, to St. Agnes to be there again. Life feels too short now to let it seep away in this pinched and graceless place.

In the settling twilight, Vito thinks of himself as a young boy on an early-summer evening in his mother's garden. He remembers her snapping a long pole bean in two and holding it out to him, one hand on his slim shoulder. He felt its dry skin and breathed in its aroma. "This is a gift from God, Vito," she said.

"Vito, you hear me?" Angie calls. She shaves a piece of pecorino into a bowl and mixes it with the torn basil leaves, the warm round potatoes, and the white pignoli. Her fingers are slick and a little sticky with the oil and garlic.

He doesn't hear her call. He is thinking now of the store. He has decided to sell it, though he has not yet told Angie.

He is selling it to an eager young Korean man and his sister. His boy Salvatore wants no part of the business. The boy thinks his father has wasted his life.

This may be the last mild evening the summer will give him before the real heat comes. Already he feels the tiring humidity. His head is light, his knees unsteady. He will stop soon and go in. He will eat and they will talk.

The mower shreds a Wrigley's wrapper, and he kneels down to pick the pieces from among the blades. Dizzy, he waits for a minute, his head bent to his chest. He leans forward on his knees, waiting for the feeling to pass.

When the sounds of the mower have stopped, Angie drains the pasta and spoons the pesto over it. She pins her hair back behind her ears.

The light is draining away from the sky. She folds two napkins, places the steaming plates on the table, and sits down to wait for him.

Then she hears the water running in the bathroom and his footsteps in the hall.

He sits down across from her. He reaches for her hand and looks into her brown eyes. "Ange," he begins to tell what has been on his mind, "I..."

And at that very moment, looking into her Vito's tired face, in their warm kitchen, with plates of Ligurian bucatini and pesto on the table she remembers what it was she had to tell him.

Philip Schumpeter Has a Beer with His Father's Ghost at a Bar in Minneapolis

Phil Schumpeter, a salesman for High and Dry Climbing Gear, is sitting alone at the bar in Brady's, a well-lit Irish bar in downtown Minneapolis. He is in the city for a business meeting.

He orders a Guinness and a bowl of stew, opens Auster's new memoir, and right then a guy takes a seat next to him and says, "You like reading that crap?"

"What?" says Phil. He thinks the guy looks like the Scred muppet from "The Land of Gorch" skit from *Saturday Night Live*.

The guy says, "Don't *what* me, Philip. I mean, don't I get a little 'Hello' or a 'How you doin', Pop?'"

Phil is flummoxed. The man sounds exactly like Scred.

"Surprised?" says the old man. "You bet your ass you are."

His hair is a mess, a two-day beard in progress, left eyelid drooping slightly. He's wearing a sky-blue hospital scrub top over a pair of baggy cutoffs.

This is his father. His father's ghost. His breath stinks like it did after the third bout of aspirational pneumonia when he had the intestinal feeding tube inserted. But the leg he had amputated when he was living in the Shady Rest Nursing Home now looks whole and just like brand new.

His father says he's in town to see his long-dead cousin Minnie. The one who was married to his Uncle Fred, the dentist from Nostrand Avenue.

"So, how's Mom doing?" Phil asks, thinking of nothing else to say. They never had much to say to each other.

"Your mother? Doing fine," the old man says, flicking his good eye at the bowl of stew.

"You want some?"

His father takes a dripping spoonful. Chewing, he says, "She's been hanging out with Stevenson and your old Aunt Goldie."

"God. Goldie? And you, what about you, how are you doing?"

"Me, I'm great. Never better. I been sort of seeing Rita."

"Rita? The one from Atlantic City?"

"Nah, Hayworth."

"You're shitting me. You and Mom split?"

"No. It's nothing like that anymore, we all kind of hang out with whoever comes around, but see—and here's the weird thing—like the other day, me and Rita are bullshitting, and all of a sudden, Eddie from Jersey City, he comes over with Truman—"

"Harry?'

"No, Capote. Anyway, they both look like they're eight years old or something, and *wham!* right away we all turn eight years old too, I mean like how we all were when we were eight. Except now we're all wearing French berets and we're talking in Gullah."

Phil takes a pull of Guinness. Offers his father some. "How the hell does that happen? You don't even know Gullah."

"Beats me. It's crazy, like, you just think of something and then you become it. We're all like, I don't know, metaphysical chameleons. They call it telegenic morphological transmogrification or something like that. It's been around a long time. Anyway, I'm really stoked. No telling what you might be like next."

"Stoked?"

"Yeah," he says. "That's the lingo there."

Then his father looks over toward the crowd smoking out by the door and he waves to this tall, slim woman. It's Minnie, who looks like she's twenty, and she waves back. He slides off the stool and pats Phil on the shoulder. "Look," he says, "I gotta go, there's a lotta people in this town happy to see me." And he starts toward the door.

"Oh, and one more thing, and this is what I came to tell you: if you ever hear anyone whispering behind their hands about Shady Acres or, you know, some place like that, when you can still walk and talk pretty good, you go find a really high cliff overlooking the deep blue sea, and you spread your arms out wide and jump the hell off. Trust me. I know whereof I speak."

And with that he spins on his heel, dressed now in a navy sports jacket and tan Dockers, a pair of Weejuns with no socks, and says, "Love ya, kid. Maybe Hoboken next time, right?"

Hodgeman's Last Thought

When Hodgeman sensed the end was near, he told Magda he loved her. "Magda, I love you," he said. And then he asked her to tell Vincenza, their daughter, to turn down the television set. He was adamant that the last thing he heard in life would not be an Arby's "We have the meats" commercial.

Would the words "I love you" be the last words he would utter? There had been others he had considered, jotting them down, mostly from intermittent Internet searches. All forgotten now, the only time he would ever need them.

More deeply troubling than what his last words would be was what his last and everlasting thought would be. Nothing enigmatic or of uncertain meaning that he didn't have time to figure out. Nothing disturbing that he could not then erase from his eternal memory.

His breath caught. It woke him. Irregular breathing: That was the sign. Was his hair neatly combed? Did his breath smell?

Would there be, in that last instant's thought, some long-hoped-for revelation? A thought, as yet, in all these years, unthought? Unexpected and pure? The one essential, universal revelation? The meaning of salvation unlocked, released finally from deep in the neurons of the timeless, ancient, lizard brain that we all will think at the end?

There were the little lies that dogged him. Would thoughts of them be the ones that could eat away at the peace of his last moment. He had never really finished *Ulysses,* though he let on he did. The cat had not really found a better life on a farm upstate. There were mean and thoughtless things he had said that might, at the final instant, flood back in a torrent of images with no way to dispel them.

When his last moment would come, when he would walk through the door, hearing the faint click of the lock at his back, when there would no longer be a chance to turn, knock softly, and ask to be admitted back in, would thoughts of kindness, selflessness, consideration, understanding, and compassion be the last *he* would remember, if only for an instant.

He was hopeful.

How could he know for certain that the last one, the very last thought, would be the one to stick with? Would he then be able to depress the morphine button, close the curtain with satisfaction, only to be wrong, only to have one last cerebral fart squeak out, one last postsynaptic word of criticism, one last neuronal drool to ablate and obliterate all the good that had come before?

Muffled voices filtered through from the other room. He closed his eyes.

Unbidden, he saw the foam-tipped waves hit the hard sand in Tofino. Felt their thud in his chest, bump hard against his ribs. Magda, her legs bathed in the surf. The setting sun at her back. The tall, black rock monuments to past time standing in the gray, watery distance...he opened his eyes and reached for the button clipped to the pillow cover, fumbled with it, depressed it once, felt the morphine haze. He pressed it again, and again.

Satisfied, he closed his eyes once more...and then...

He is walking down Fifth Avenue. The air is clear, crisp. It is fall. A tall, attractive woman is coming toward him. A smart leather briefcase is slung over the shoulder of her dark navy-blue business suit. Her heels click on the pavement. A silky white blouse. Its fabric pulled tightly across the soft swell of her breasts. The hint of a nipple. Only feet away. She looks up at him and her hand moves quickly, instinctively, to pull at the suit jacket, to cover her chest from his fleeting, intrusive, irretrievable, shameful gaze.

"Die, asshole," she says.

Helen Burnside, Prom Queen

Helen Burnside had decided to leave New York. From her window in Brooklyn Heights, she had seen the two towers collapse and the too-late jets flying in tight formation through the clear September blue.

She despaired. New York was no longer where she wanted to be. She sold her parents' old three-bedroom co-op, stored her furniture and her watercolors, and carried a suitcase, her paint box, her worries, and a carton of books to Penn Station.

On the train out of Manhattan, she sat, unsettled, eating nothing, stopping and starting to read the book in her lap.

Helen's cousin, Bea Longfellow, a retired New York City schoolteacher, lived in an apartment in a small town on the coast north of Boston. She had an extra bedroom to offer Helen. The offer was sincere, and Helen accepted, even if it was not well-considered. Bea had voted for Bush, and this fact was like an uninvited dinner guest between them. One who breathed heavily and sucked his teeth after every course.

Helen first saw Mackenzie in the park not far from Bea's.

He was alone, hitting tennis balls on the shaded tennis court, sweating, and determined. He was tall, slender, and self-contained in a gracious way. He looked to be around Helen's age.

In Brooklyn, Helen had lived near a park where she practiced tai chi on the Esplanade with a group of other women who also were single by choice.

One morning, after his workout, Mac sat down on the bench near to where Helen was sitting. They talked casually about exercise, politics, and the hardcover she was reading. He had taken a lease on a cottage up the hill. Like her, he was an immigrant from the city he loved but felt the need to leave.

Helen began to look forward to seeing him. Attracted in a simple, uncomplicated way. In time, she found herself planning some of her days around his schedule.

Bea asked if Helen was being naïve and impulsive. She herself had seen the man in the park and was wary of what he was doing there day after day, never with anyone else. You had to wonder. And you had to look out for yourself.

"Face it, Helen, us grandmother types had our shot. It's over. You only get one chance to be the prom queen. Now we have to settle for doing the right thing, or at least looking like we are."

One afternoon, Helen walked up the hill to Mackenzie's place with him. He paused on the path, the rust-and-gray-streaked quarry wall behind him. He turned to her. She looked up at him. He took her arm. Her heart boomed. He told her that he was on estrogen therapy, had been for a few months. Awaiting sex-reassignment surgery.

"Oh my God," she said. "I mean, I don't mean that in a bad way. I mean, I don't know what I mean." She began to cry. He put his arm around her.

"How about some tea?" he said.

Some nights Helen stayed at Mac's. Nina Simone records. Coltrane. Warm goat cheese salads. They read together. Helen tended to her brushes, her paints. Mackenzie strung his racquets and wrote ad copy for the summer IKEA catalogue.

They talked. Gender gap among artists, friends at Cooper Union, intersectionality, whatever that meant, and living to be the age your parents were in the photos of them in your wallet.

In November, Helen painted a portrait of Mackenzie. Another in January. Snow clung in clumps to the limbs of the naked oaks.

They both cut their hair, and Helen painted one of the two of them nose-to-nose. She moved her books onto his shelves.

A part of her, a big part, wished nothing would ever change between them, that this feeling would last forever.

She spent more time with Mac than with Bea. She painted each day. Working now with acrylics and palette knives. Feeling the freedom of a new, aggressive form and medium.

When she told Bea she'd be moving back to New York, Bea said, "It's that man, isn't it?"

In New York, Mac recovered from the surgeries. Helen's portraits were installed in a one-woman show in Brooklyn. She drank peach Bellinis. She wore black a lot.

Mackenzie returned to work full-time. Played at the Midtown Tennis Club. Learned to rumba. Wore red a lot. She started anti-androgens and considered implants.

Helen opened a gallery in Tribeca. She watched Mackenzie play. They met for dinners. Films at the Sunshine on Houston Street. Found friends in the Movement.

Mac's new apartment in Chelsea overlooked the water. Helen's was a well-lit loft in SoHo. Time passed, and almost without notice, they seemed to drift apart.

Then late one evening, Helen called.

At lunch the next day, Helen despaired. Sales had dropped. Her muse no longer answered her emails. An *ARTnews* critic called her work stale and monotonous. She knew he was just feeling threatened by her. Maybe both were true.

Mac said she felt lonely and isolated and shunned. At the office, men and women stared at her with narrow lips, over cubicle walls, while they ate their hummus wraps at their desks. No one said a word when HR and security trailed her as she carried her pens, plants, and coffee mug to the elevator.

"Oh, Mac," Helen said. "I don't know what to do. What now?"

"I don't know. I feel lost."

Passersby, looking in through the café window, might have seen the tall, slender woman with a straight back and long brown hair get up from the other side of the table and sit down on the banquette beside a woman in a black tunic.

They might then have seen the tall woman gently place her hand in the other woman's open palm. Seen them move closer together, both faces now lit by the light coming in through the window on the avenue.

My Lunch with Revson

Revson, seeing a table free, hurried ahead of me to a sun-drenched table by the window facing 10th Avenue. He took a seat. The table still had the lunch dishes left by the previous diners. Two five-dollar bills were under a white coffee mug.

The Empire Diner on 10th and 22nd Street was not a seat-yourself place, but Revson made his own rules.

He was a balding, unapologetic iconoclast. He reveled in this as might a dog rolling in the scent of rabbit scat in a warm, grassy patch of sun.

Word had it that he was related to the Long Island Revlon Revsons, though he never spoke of it, and there were unverified rumors that his mother was Eartha Kitt, the result of the long-running, well-known affair she'd had with Charles Revson.

I became obsessed with researching his family history, checking newspaper archives, birth records, even investing a small amount of cash in a deep-web genealogy website. He was nowhere to be found in the official family tree.

His name was Revson R. Revson. He was a wisp of a man. His back was as straight as the Long Island Expressway. He wore threadbare brown tweeds, sweater vests, and hand-tied, patterned bowties.

For some in our small circle of friends, it was as much a burden as an entertainment to pay rapt attention to his stories, though that was not the case for me. While they thought him often crass and ill-informed, I found him to be a delightful companion. He could offer, with relish and absolute conviction, wondrous, insightful thoughts to any conversation, no matter how abstruse, technical, or arcane it might be.

I recall when I first met him. He was at a table in McSorley's near Cooper Union. The table was long, and he was perched in the center, eating a thick liverwurst and onion sandwich, and talking with a few men who were nursing pints of Guinness. You might remember that McSorley's was, at that time, a women-only-by-invitation bar.

Revson was in the midst of a peroration about, of all things, the underlying political-economic provenance of *The Wizard of Oz*. "You know, of course," he said, sounding much like a young John Houseman, "the whole film was based upon the debate in the late 1890s over whether or not to replace gold with silver as the coin of the realm."

As evidence, he proffered that Oz was the obvious choice for the name of the false wizard. "You see," he said, "gold, as you know, is listed in the periodic table of elements as *O-Z*. Need I say more?"

I found him fascinating. He knew so much and shared it so freely.

As for the two fives on the table, I fully expected that he. being a bit of a skinflint, might pocket the bills and then offer up one for a tip at the end of the meal. This may have happened. I don't know. For, just at that moment, in walked Wallace, an actor friend. Revson excitedly waived him over just as the busboy came to clear the table.

Revson and Wallace had become acquainted through a chance meeting in the waiting room of a Park Avenue psychotherapist with whom they had back-to-back appointments. Wallace had been late for his appointment, and Revson was early. They struck up a conversation and a loose friendship.

As Wallace was about to pass our table, Revson gestured and bade him to join us. "Sit, sit, please," he said. Wallace eyed me and slid into the booth.

We spent a few moments with "Hello" and "How are things?" All the while, Wallace was looking around the long, narrow diner, perhaps for an empty table.

"Revson and I were just talking about New York, how it's changing," I said to Wallace, drawing him into the conversation. "You've lived here all your life. Am I right?" He nodded in agreement. "Well, Revson was just observing that he has too. In fact, if I can remember his words exactly, he said—and Revson, correct me if I am wrong—he said, 'I've lived in this city all my life. I grew up on the Upper East Side. And when I was ten years old, I was rich, I was an aristocrat. Riding around in taxis, surrounded by comfort, and all I thought about was art and music. Now, I'm thirty-six, and all I think about is women.'"

At that, Wallace's face reddened. He stood and looked down at us. "You are a fool," he said, looking straight at me. "That is the most ridiculous thing I have ever heard. And my dear Revson, you are an even bigger fool."

"That little speech of yours," he sputtered, "comes from my film *My Dinner with Andre*. I wrote that, you idiot. I wrote every one of those words, except for the last. The last line, you ignominious idiot, is 'Now, I'm thirty-six, and all I think about is *money*—not women."

He looked from one of us to the other. "You are both colossal fools," he said, and he left the diner.

Revson rolled his eyes. "Pay him no heed," he said. "Self-important, arrogant people have no capacity for having a good time. They are simply devoid of a single kernel of joy! You no doubt saw his devious behavior on display in *The Princess Bride*. Let us order. I believe I will have the tomato and olive tarte tatin with the crab cakes rémoulade. How about you?"

The Good Life of Avrum and Chava

Avrum and Chava live in a three-bedroom, two-and-a-half-bath home in North Ossining, a town not far from the max-security prison down by the river. They have two and a half acres, iron gates, their own well, and deer fences protecting their garden.

Avrum is a retired lawyer and Chava is a former social worker for the department of corrections at Sing Sing, where they met.

For thirty years together, they have led cautious, well-organized lives. They grow their own fruits and vegetables, use no plastics, and stopped using aluminum pans and deodorants years ago. They don't own cell phones or a microwave. Their home is rid of mold, lead, polyfluorocarbonate aromatics, errant asbestos fibers, and radon.

They look like well-pressed waifs. Each weighs thirty pounds less than their recommended body weight. They consume no more than 800 calories per day and walk eight miles each day to remain in strict calorie balance.

They are new-age vegans. Macrobiotics, fermentationists. Their yoga instructor finds them existentially intimidating.

When they turned fifty, they both assessed their risks, and he had a prophylactic prostatectomy and she a hysterectomy and double mastectomy.

They are friendly and sociable, literate, kind, careful, and caring people.

One Thursday evening, they are heading north on the Henry Hudson Parkway after attending the concluding performance of the entire Ring Cycle at Lincoln Center when they are sideswiped by a gypsy cab with its lights off and are sent careening into and over the guardrail. When their front and side airbags deployed, given their light weight and small size, they are crumpled and almost instantly suffocated.

At the moment of their death, they are surrounded by a halo of warm, mauve light.

A reassuringly backlit vision of a fifty-something woman with neatly trimmed hair, a string of pearls, and a white pantsuit appears to them.

She speaks slowly in a vaguely Midwestern accent. "Don't be alarmed," she tells them. "Just try to relax. I promise, you will be all right."

They look unsure.

"You are not dying. You have been granted a reprieve; a temporarily permanent stay of execution, so to speak; a lifetime dispensation."

"Why us?" Chava asks.

"To tell you the truth, we don't offer this to everyone. You've both lived exemplary lives of service, positive thoughts, and quiet restraint. Model citizens. No felonies. We are trying to encourage more of that."

"Wait, are we dead? Is this Heaven?" asks Avrum.

"No, not exactly. And we did away with the heaven concept eons ago. It was one of those social engineering experiments we tried, but it just wasn't giving us the kind of results we were looking for. You know, debauchery, gluttony, sloth, sexual harassment, war, drones, all of that persisted despite our best intentions. Dangling the prospect of heaven never had any effect."

"What if we take this offer, what do we have to do? What happens next?" asks Avrum.

"Well, nothing changes. Everything stays the same. You just agree to maintain your lifestyle. You stay forever just as you were fifteen minutes ago, before the crash. We need folks like you to set an example for other couples."

"Nothing changes? Our bank account?"

"The same."

"Investments?"

"Same."

"Health insurance?"

"Same. My God, think of all the books, the movies, the bar mitzvahs, the weddings. No pressure to do anything you don't want to *forever*. You just agree to let us use your names and faces in a new Internet lifestyle advertising campaign we're starting. Think of it. Your home will be free and clear when the mortgage expires. Of course, you'll need to have the wiring upgraded and the appliances repaired, replace the boiler, replace the roof when needed— you know, the usual maintenance every 150 years or so."

She senses hesitation.

"I know this will work for you. For you both. What do I have to do to make this happen for you?"

Silence.

"Look, not to rush you, but if just put your thumb prints right here, you are free to go. You'll never see me again."

Chava and Avrum look at each other. He reaches gently for her hand. "I'm in," he says.

"Great, Avrum. This is so you!"

"Wait," Chava says. "What if we decide *not* to take the offer? I mean, what happens if we say no?"

"Well, no one has ever actually said no before. I guess you just get the usual, you know, one last meal of your choosing and then, well, it's curtains. *Finito.*"

"A last meal?"

"Yes."

"Chava, what are you saying?" Avrum whispers.

"Wait. What could we have?"

"Anything!"

"Anything?"

Chava lowers her eyes in thought. "Well," she says quietly. "Could I have three eggs, scrambled wet, home fries, and wheat— no, wait, make that pumpernickel—toast with butter?"

Avrum looks at her. He is aghast. "Chava. No," he says.

"Will that be all?" the woman asks.

Avrum shakes his head, tells her nothing for him. He looks at Chava.

"Can I have a side of bacon too?" she says.

"Of course."

"And a regular coffee, light and sweet?"

"Chava, please."

She looks into Avrum's warm, gray eyes, smoothes her hand against his rough cheek. "Oh, Avrum," she tells him. "I'm sorry. I love you, I do. I've had a good life."

THE LAST DAYS OF ELSA AND ALBERT
AT THE CAPUTH SUMMER HOUSE

Elsa Einstein stands on her front porch, waiting for the mail. It is a morning in mid-September, and the oaks down the hill along the lake are beginning to redden. A cool breeze stirs the folds of her skirt. She fills her lungs deeply with coolness and watches the breeze darken the surface of the gray-blue Templiner See as it flows past Caputh north toward Potsdam.

When the postman has gone, she retrieves the bundle of mail from the postbox.

A letter has come for Albert. He is in his study. She waits until he comes out for lunch to give it to him.

"A letter for you," she says. She passes it to him across the table. He looks at it.

"Are you feeling unwell?" she asks.

"I am well," he tells her. "Why do you ask me this?"

"You got a letter from our Dr. Freud. Should I not worry that something is wrong, that something is troubling you?"

"It is not your worry, Elsa," he tells her. "Are not we *all* troubled now?"

"Will you show it to me? The letter?"

He looks at her, pondering what to say. Then says nothing and returns to his study, only to come back out after it has gotten dark.

Elsa has made dinner for the two of them. She leans toward him across the table, waiting for him to speak.

"I wrote to Dr. Freud," he tells her, "and he has answered me. That is all. It is not about you, nor about me. I asked him a question. I asked how we might, together, as men of learning and intellect, find a way, after all of the suffering we have endured, of helping to deliver mankind from the menace of another war."

"And what did he say to you?"

"He despaired. He said that we are caught between Eros and death instincts. He has little hope for civilization."

"And you are surprised by his response?"

"It is not what I expected."

"Albert, please, you are a smart man. We both know that men do stupid things. Hurtful and sometimes horrible things. They cheat on their wives. They gamble away the family's earnings. They say mean and nasty things. They ignore the feelings of others. They seldom think of the less fortunate. They don't consider the consequences of their actions. But not all men are like that."

"I know that."

"Of course you do. You are a good man. But you are a theoretician. Your mind wanders among the unknowable, while the knowable is standing right there in front of you."

"What are you saying?"

"Albert, not all people have the time to think like you do. They need to sweep the floors. Make dinner. Patch the roof. They are not writing letters. They have other things to worry about. Thinking, like you and your friend Sigmund can do, is not even on their to-do list in a year."

"I know that too."

"And do you know how many people there are in the world, Albert?"

"Two billion."

"Yes, two billion hungry, frightened souls. And how many of them are capable of starting wars or even of thinking about such things? How many? I can tell you. Less than ten people in the whole world. Maybe less than five. And now think of this, Albert—how many of those two billion people have the power to *prevent* a war if the five want to *start* one? I'll tell you. None. Not one. Not even you. And how many of the two billion died in the war? Forty million. *Forty million*, Albert, every one of whom would have stopped the war in a breath if they could have."

"Yes. You are right."

"But, Albert, tell me, how many of those five self-centered powerful men would have acted to stop the war *before* it started? What little would it have taken for them to do that? And now, let me ask you, my dear husband, how many of those five died in the war?"

He shakes his head.

"Exactly. None. And in the letters you and Sigmund have written back and forth and all of the talk about your theories and such, what have you come to? I'll tell you what. You both agree that, in the end, no one can stop warlike men from whipping up the people who are dependent, cowering, and easily swayed to pick up arms and kill and die, all of which brings unheard-of and obscene wealth and power to those warmongering power-obsessed few. Not even the League of Nations."

"Yes."

"All we can hope for is that we poor human beings, in the years to come, in what we both know now is only the early dawn of our collective existence, evolve a civilization in which the love of life and peace and the repugnance of war somehow become the unquestioned cultural norm and are written into our very genes. I guarantee you, Albert, that neither you and I nor Sigmund and his dear wife Martha will ever live to see that time.

"If you had asked me, Albert, I would have told you that the only way to see anything approaching an end to war is that if the people, the proletariat, become convinced that the only honorable thing to do is to give the commanders-in-chief and ten of their closest military and economic advisors the privilege of standing in the front of the line or at ground zero or whatever you call it with big red targets of honor on their chests and lead their soldiers into battle. To take the first bullet. The first grenade. Anything less than that will do nothing."

"You know that will never happen."

"Of course not. Then, Albert, look around you. *We* are wearing the targets. *We* are living in fear of what will happen to us next. This is no time for theorizing and thinking about things until they wither and die under the weight of your heavy thoughts. It is time now for us to pack our things. To leave while we can. Not the time for more letters or more talking."

Albert is quiet. He goes to his room.

Two months later, on December 6th, Albert packs his manuscripts and his violin. Elsa, with her one suitcase, and one for him, waits on the porch for him. He locks the door behind him, and they take the train from Caputh to Antwerp and never return.

THE COMPANY

Fanny Merriweather is soft-spoken. Trim. Well-dressed. My brother's wife. She wears belted skirts and medium-heel Cole Haan pumps. She must have several pairs of them. Or she likely purchases a new pair before the one she has been wearing looks worn. All of them are of a color called oxblood, if that name is still in use. They are always well polished, and all have leather soles and heels made of a material that is clearly not rubber.

Nothing about her would draw any attention. No ostentation of any sort. No indication that a risk, fashion or otherwise, of any order higher than occasionally crossing against the green would ever be undertaken. Certainly no social risk. No political stance expressed that opposed a commonly agreed-upon norm.

She calls to mind a slim stalk of winter wheat. One stalk, indistinguishable from the hundreds of others in a field, waiting, green, near-dormant throughout the cold months, awaiting a return to vitality and growth in the spring. Enduring a period of personal solitude amongst a crowd of indistinguishable similars.

Hers is the look of muted heather and woolens. The look of old wealth, though I know nothing of her financial position. The look of comfortable socks, tweeds, and natural fabrics you might envision while reading the novels of Thomas Hardy or Edith Wharton.

When we dine together on occasion, she might order the baked haddock or the pasta of the day, or more often, she'd order what my brother had just ordered. She has never ventured into sashimi, say, or unagi, shawarma, kimchi, vindaloo, or baba ghanoush, though I know she has traveled widely in the world.

I have never seen her in any state other than unruffled. She is not prone to fits of passion or to indiscretion. I cannot envision her engaged in a flirtation, a dalliance, or a one-nighter in Baltimore, much less an actual affair. She apparently passed through midlife without missing a step or looking up old high school boyfriends or buying a Harley-Davidson.

There is something, though. Something too measured. Too neatly ironed and folded about her.

I keep waiting for a revelation of some deep-hidden darkness. For a secret past to emerge in a slipped word or a creased and faded note fallen accidentally from her wallet or a wry smile at a line in a movie, as if she had once been in a similar situation, in a predicament that only a Nikita, an Emma Peel, or a Dominika Egorova character might find herself caught in. A hint of a hidden fissure in an otherwise well-concealed life.

She seems like someone kept in a witness-protection program since adolescence. Someone whose name was changed, and who had to learn to root for the Chicago Cubs instead of the New York Yankees. Someone trained to be unprovoked. Unprovocable. Implacable. Avoiding expressions of pity, sadness, ecstasy, consternation, confusion, empathy, condescension, or suspicion. Any of these.

I have come to suspect, with almost no justification, that she was once an agent of the CIA. Recruited, plucked out of Harvard or Yale as so many were in the late sixties. Young men and women who studied hard, got decent grades, and were identified by a well-connected professor for ineluctable qualities of rigor, academicism, unquestioning patriotism, interiority, intensity, and detachment.

Has she ever poisoned someone, plotted the overthrow of a dictator or a communist leader? Can she snap a person's neck with her bare hands? Has she used code and encrypted messaging devices? Kept a cyanide tablet in her purse? Taken a lover in Paraguay? Perhaps a woman who tried to turn her and whom she had in turn tried to recruit as an asset. A woman who was married to the defense minister, who was plotting a military takeover of the government. Sex and spy craft seem inseparable.

From whence comes my suspicion. I don't know. Perhaps it is from my obsessive reading of Mailer, le Carré, and others of the same sort. Books my brother often recommends to me. Perhaps it is only a fiction of my own that I created from what little I heard or pieced from ill-founded, erroneous assumptions. Perhaps it is only what I want to believe for reasons of which I am not aware.

I know she worked for the USAID. A mid-level position. Moved from place to place with my brother and the two children. Pictures of her in South America. In Eritrea. Disbursing funds for development. Moving easily between embassy offices and home government agencies, banks, and NGOs, learning only enough of the language to seem harmless and friendly. Perhaps monitoring the Russians and the Chinese. And then the year in Congo. Years in which the USAID and the CIA were joined at the hip. How could she not have been involved? Could not have known what she was associated with? Was she merely an unknowing pawn doing good work for a bad, if not immoral, arm of the state? To whom was she beholden? Who gave her her orders?

We're having dinner with them tonight. We haven't seen Fanny and my brother for over a year. They've been living in Miami. COVID restrictions and our own calculus of infection risk have kept us apart.

Now we're all vaccinated.

I expect that when I open our door, she will smile, standing a shade behind my brother, and I will smile back. Her smile seems shy and somehow calculated to me. As if she is simultaneously smiling and thinking quickly of something to say to me. Something witty to which she knows I will respond equally quickly and wittily. Or testing me in some way. Am I a suspect of some kind? Nevertheless, this is how we have come to talk to each other. An argot that lends itself to friendly, diversionary, insubstantial communication. A measure of casual, risk-averse comradery. Though, I must say, I enjoy it greatly.

My brother hands me a bottle of wine, a pleasant-looking rosé from a small vineyard outside of Rome, New York, which we will open and share with a mild cheddar and a basket of Triscuits and Wheat Thins.

Looking at Fanny, her calm and pleasant demeanor, which I have not seen in so long, taking her coat, I begin to question my motivation. Could it be driven by a sense of jealousy or of prurience? Wishing her to fulfill some fantasy of my own making. Perhaps the calculation, the intrigue, is of my own doing and through which I might be hiding something. Or, or...as I place the bottle of wine on the coffee table along with the wine glasses, I glance at the copy of *Harlot's Ghost* I have been reading, sent to me by my brother, and a thought comes to me. The books. The intrigue. The pictures of her. Never of my brother. Not one of him. In all those years.

He is the one. The spy. My brother. *My brother!*

Allie Goes to a Communion Party

When Allie was in the third grade at P.S. 89 in the Bronx, he was invited to Annmarie Santopietro's party. his mother walked him to the apartment not far from theirs, though not in the same neighborhood. Theirs was in the Projects, groups of apartment buildings in New York built in the late forties and early fifties providing a working-class housing mostly for young families with children all about Allie's age.

Annmarie lived in the Italian neighborhood. At least, that's what Allie's parents called it. What his mother called it. It was on the other side of the elementary school. Closer to Allerton Avenue, where there were banks and barbershops, restaurants, clothing stores, and a theater.

His mother waited until someone answered the door. A round woman, soft-cheeked, with a billowy chest, gray hair, and an apron tied over a black dress opened the door. "Come in," she said.

His mother left him there. She said she'd be back to pick him up at the end of the party. The woman took his hand, said goodbye to his mother, and closed the door. His mother, he heard, was saying "You be good" to him as the door was shut behind him.

Annmarie was there. In a frilled white dress, white anklets, and polished white shoes.

The apartment was filled with people. People everywhere. Cooking, talking, eating, drinking, running, sitting, standing, crawling, laughing. Sweet onions, garlic, sweat, cigarettes. Unfamiliar voices. Music. The sound of it all seemed to get steadily louder and louder as he stood in the living room.

Annmarie tossed the gift he brought her onto the living room couch, piled high with coats, hats, and packages.

There were young men in loose-fitting black suits and white shirts buttoned to the neck holding glasses filled with red wine. They were in the living room, talking. They smiled when they saw him. Their faces were tanned, their thick black hair was combed back from their foreheads, and their hands were strong and rough, muscular. These men looked like the kind of men Allie's mother would pull him away from and cross the street to avoid, whether they were walking toward them or coming out of a store or even just standing on the sidewalk, smoking, talking, and laughing like they were there, in the living room, gesturing with their hands, up close in one another's faces.

Women, many of them, were in the kitchen wearing thick-soled shoes like his own grandmother and aunts wore, opening and closing the icebox, mixing bowls full of meat with their hands, slicing loaves of bread as long as an arm, and lifting spoonfuls of hot red sauce to their lips from pots on the stove.

Beside the couch was a large, polished, wooden Victrola cabinet. The sounds of music coming from it and the voices, along with the clatter of dishes and silverware, filled the whole apartment.

Annmarie's room was in the back of the apartment. It was bright, with pink curtains on the windows. Three of her cousins were there. They were all dressed alike in fitted white suits, carnations in their lapels. There were no other children from his class there. He was the only one.

He was wearing a blue-striped polo shirt tucked into his short pants, and brown shoes and socks. No one said a word. He looked at them and they looked at him.

The walls were white, and above Annmarie's bed hung a large wooden cross. He had seen crosses before. Certainly. Thin gold ones. On necklaces. But none were anything like this one. On this one was the long, thin, nearly bare body of Jesus. Allie knew that. He was dying, it seemed. His arms were splayed out, and his head had fallen to one side. Blood dripped from his forehead, his side, and from the spikes driven through his palms, and his eyes looked upward.

No one ever told Allie not to look at a cross or a Jesus or anything like that, it just felt to him as if there must be something forbidden about doing that. Or if it were a sin. They never talked about sins at home. They talked about being kosher and what not to do on Friday nights and Saturdays. That was it. There was no talk about Jesus. But the feeling he had looking at the Jesus on the cross on the wall above the bed was itself probably forbidden.

Annmarie lived in her grandmother's apartment. Her parents lived upstairs with her younger brother, and her aunts lived in the apartment on the first floor. Allie was used to visiting his grandparents every Sunday in Manhattan. First visiting with one of them and then leaving and going to see the other grandparents, and then going home to their own apartment.

Before long, at the party, everyone was called to the table. The children at one. The adults at another. Large bowls of spaghetti, covered in a red sauce. Steaming. Meatballs as big as apples. Grated cheese. Peppers. Parsley. Bread and butter. He had never seen as much food at one time in one place.

One of the cousins reached for his hand and bowed his head. Everyone around the table did that. He did too. And the grandfather thanked God for the food and for the family and for the children making their communion, which he had never heard of before. He raised his head only when they did. This was, no doubt, another sin, or maybe more than one. He didn't know.

One of Annmarie's aunts tucked a napkin into his shirt. "Eat," she said, prodding his shoulder. He did, sucking in the strands of spaghetti, biting into a warm meatball. This was an absolute sin.

No doubt. He had never before eaten a single bite of food outside of his house or at one of his relatives' houses. This food was *treif*. Unkosher. Unkosher food of any kind is absolutely forbidden. It was delicious. He knew it was wrong. The wrongest thing he had ever done. He knew it.

After they ate, they left the table and the grandfather went over to change the record on the Victrola. He held the record by its edges, sliding it slowly into its paper sleeve in a large cardboard album book, and then he dusted off another and placed it onto the turntable. Everyone crowded around to watch him lower the needle onto the record. They pushed against one another to get close. He turned up the volume. The record hissed, and the music began again.

Allie was elbowed back against the cluttered couch. The cushions were high, covered with coats and other things, and he climbed up on top to make room. On top of the pile.

He felt the records break beneath him a moment before he heard them crack. He could not stop himself from sinking deeper into the stack of albums below him. He didn't know how many records were under him. Breaking. Shattering. The jagged pieces grating against one another.

He felt his face burning. His ears ringing. His stomach clenching.

He needed to leave, to go home somehow. He got off the couch slowly and looked to the door. And then, before he could take a step, the grandmother brought out the cake and lit the candles. A tall, white-frosted cake. Everyone rushed back to the table. He went with them. They sang and clapped.

He looked at all the faces of the family around the table, looking at their eyes, thinking that one may have seen or heard what he had done. They were eating big slices of cake, talking, and licking the white icing from their lips and chins.

He wanted to sink beneath the table. To leave. To crawl away. To be home.

He said nothing.

When his mother came for him, he said goodbye and he left with her. And they walked home.

He knew, though, that when the coats were picked up and they saw the grandfather's broken records they would ask everyone who had done that. And no one would say they had. Because it was he who had broken them. And what would they do then?

He knew he would never ever tell his mother or his father. Not about the Jesus on the cross that he had stared at or the bowed heads and prayer they said around him. Not about the meatballs and the cheese on the spaghetti that he had eaten or the records or anything.

And regardless of how good he would be from then on, how many punishments he would deserve and receive, or how many years would pass, he would remember that day and regret what he had done at the party. As irrational as it may sound, he knew that one day, a punishment would come, for any or all of it. The worst of all was walking away from what he had done. Walking away and not, right then, right there, saying, "I did that. I broke the grandfather's records, and I am sorry. I am sorry for what I did."

DIALOGUE ON THE WAY TO GRANDMA'S HOUSE

Mira is in the back seat of the Volvo. She is in her car seat. Her face is in the rearview mirror. I can see her eating a peanut butter sandwich. She does not like it cut in half, neither horizontally nor diagonally. And she likes the thin brown crust on.

"Why are we going to Grandma's house?"

"Because it is Mother's Day."

"But she is not my mother."

"No, but she is my mother."

"When is Grandmother's Day?"

"I don't know."

"Could we go see her tomorrow?"

"I don't think so."

"Why?"

"Because you have to go to school."

"Why do I have to go to school?"

"Because you like school."

"What if I didn't like it?"

"But you do."

"What if I didn't?"

"You would still have to go."

"What if you die when I am in school?"

"That is not going to happen."

"But what if?"

"Honey, it is not going to happen."

"What if I die when I go to school?"

"You are not going to die when you go to school."

"How do you know?"

"I just know. You are a little girl."

"But what if?"

"It is not going to happen."

"Would you be sad?"

"I would be so sad that I would cry forever."

"What is forever?"

"A long, long time."

"How long?"

"The longest, longest time in the whole world."

"In the universe?"

"Yes. In the universe."

"When will the universe die?"

"Never."

"How do you know?"

"Einstein told me."

"How does he know?"

"He worked it out in school."

"Oh."

THE GENIE

On his way home from work each evening, Wilson picked up takeout and a copy of the *Post-Standard*. He'd eat and read it at the kitchen table under the anemic light of a flickering florescent fixture he had long planned to replace.

The work he'd brought home with him would wait until after he finished the paper. He underlined articles of interest, cutting some out neatly with an X-Acto knife, intending to send them to his sister in Fredonia, and then he'd get to circling with a red marker each promising WSM singles ad in the "Plenty-O-Fish" personals column.

Wilson worked at Genie, Inc., a small human genome research and development startup on the outskirts of Syracuse. The company was home to a select group of young, smart tech grads, and each hoped one day they'd get bought out by a giant biotech and make a million and retire to Tahiti.

One woman who posted an ad in the "Just Looking/Not Desperate" section and who was about his own age, perhaps a little older, met him after work for a drink at Café Kubal, an all-night coffee shop on James Street near the mall.

She was an instructor at the university, working on her dissertation in Comparative Eastern Literature. Her thesis was on a content analysis of Bhutanese-Nepali literary criticism before and after 1999, the signal year that television broadcasts first came to Bhutan.

Her name was Cymbal.

It was originally Cynthia Orenstein, but she changed it when she turned twenty-one, soon after a dream she had in which it was revealed that she was, in a past life, the daughter of a simple and poor Tibetan farm couple.

Wilson did not believe in reincarnation, and he told her so. However, each time he saw her, he believed more and more in the magical Cymbal. There were secrets of Tibetan mountain agriculture she knew that could not be found in any textbook. She knew the names of all of the wives her husband had and the colors of the scarves they wore so that he could tell them all apart.

He was almost convinced. More so, though, he was intrigued by the possibility that there might be some telltale epigenetic evidence of her Tibetan past hidden deep within the unseen strands of her DNA.

One evening while they were having a late dinner at his place, when she left the table to go to the bathroom, he picked up her napkin and swabbed it along the edge of her teacup and slipped it into the plastic sample bag he had in his pocket for just such an opportunity.

The next day at work, he placed tiny squares of her napkin into an array of test vials, and he ran the batch through the company's mitochondrial genetic sequencing analyzer and human genome research database.

He was standing, he realized, at the nexus of science and séance. If it all worked out, there was, no doubt, a Nobel Prize in this for him.

It took several days for the base pair sequencing to be completed and several more for the bio-geo-ethnographic report to be returned from the scanner.

In the meantime, over savory native dishes like chana ko tarkari and keema bhutuwa, which she cooked for him in his kitchen, he became more and more unsure of the objective reality he believed in, and more and more sure that there were things in this world that he might never ever come to understand.

He was enthralled with the stories of her past and enamored with her present, intoxicated by her confident self-knowledge, and captivated by her capacity for unconditional love.

What was real to her was becoming reality to him.

And when the test results arrived in a large manila envelope, he set it aside, unopened. For weeks, he was tormented. He questioned his motives. He was deeply in love with Cymbal and she with him. How, though, would he feel about her DNA? How could he explain to her what he had done? Invading and violating her body by taking her DNA, her essence, and hiding that from her.

One weekend when Cymbal was at a conference in San Diego, he opened the envelope.

In the unsparing light at his kitchen table, the results were clear.

There were no Tibetan genes to be found. No Bhutani or Nepali. No Eurasian, No Mongol or South Asian; no East Asian, nothing even close. There were only Eastern European alleles with traces of North African ancestry. Nothing even remotely Tibetan.

He creased the sheets of paper down the middle and carefully tore them in half. He slid them into the envelope, and he secreted it in a drawer beneath some old socks and underwear he no longer wore. He vowed never to look at them again and never ever to show them to her.

When the last of their three children graduated from college, Wilson and Cymbal decided to downsize to an old shepherd's cottage in the High Sierra mountains. They'd be cultivating yartsa gunbu, the rare and costly Tibetan aphrodisiac harvested from the parasitic caterpillar mummy fungus.

In cleaning out his drawerful of ragged socks, there was the envelope he had hidden away. He had not looked at in over twenty years.

He opened the envelope. The printout was gone. In its place, on a small sheet of college-ruled notepaper, were written, in Cymbal's simple script and firm, confident hand, the words of the Buddha: "What you are is what you have been. What you'll be is what you do now."

An Early Supper at the Café Le Gamin

I sat at a table in the Café Le Gamin on 10th Avenue and 17th Street.

Marchant, the proprietor of the café, with whom I had become well acquainted, and with whom, on occasion, I attended the bicycle races along the river, approached the table.

When I had arrived, he had been leaning back against the half-wall separating the kitchen from the dining area. It was early. Too early for New York people to have supper—those who worked uptown until eight or nine and lived in one-bedroom walk-ups in Chelsea or the West Village south of 23rd, where you could still occasionally find a place for under two thousand a month. And where, in the hours after dark, after the meat-packing businesses had darkened and the long trucks had left, narrow-hipped women and men in short skirts and high heels walked the streets or stood with long legs outstretched, smoking on shadowed corners under the elevated railway and bending over to look in the rolled-down windows of the cars slowing along the curb.

Marchant carried two glasses and an open bottle of a St. Amour Beaujolais. He set the cork and bottle down and placed one glass in front of me.

"May I sit?" he asked. I nodded.

He took the chair opposite me so that he retained a view of the kitchen. I had an unhindered view of the street. I could see the park across the way. A vest-pocket park created, like others in the city, in small vacant lots during the Lindsay administration.

Marchant raised his glass to me.

In the years before Giuliani chained and locked shut the park gates to keep unsavory characters out, I would sit on benches there with friends and smoke and talk books and writing. The Clement C. Moore Park has a sign now that says "No adults admitted unless accompanied by a child under 7." It's hard to say whether or not that keeps away or encourages the unsavory characters.

"Mr. Bergman," said Marchant. His voice was hoarse. Perhaps he had been cheering at the bicycle races that afternoon, but I had not seen him there. "I have seen to it that your soup and fresh bread will be out in a moment."

"Thank you," I said. Marchant was not a gregarious man. He seemed weary. Wearier than when I had seen him last.

The M11 stopped at the opposite corner in front of the laundromat. The bus kneeled, and a woman with a Burberry scarf around her neck and a cat carrier stepped to the curb. Spring had been slow in coming.

"Are you comfortable? I can put up the heat if you wish."

I told him no. There was no need. I heard the shushing of the bus through the open window as it righted itself.

"Very well," he said. "And your wife. She is well?"

"Yes," I said.

"She is a lovely woman. A woman of great taste and beauty. Will she be joining you this evening?"

"No. It is Wednesday. We have our meals apart on Wednesdays. She works late and then sees some friends of hers for drinks. I must soon get to work myself."

I write in the evenings. Most evenings. The room I rent by the month on West Street is most quiet in the evening. I have found that I work best after an early supper. I work until I think I have written a draft that is not terrible and then I leave it to sort itself out a bit before returning to it the next evening.

Some evenings, though, when I find the words will not come, I put on my hat and walk along the river instead. I find that helpful. As I watch the current shift the boats on their mooring lines, a thought, a name, a phrase will enter my mind, and I walk back to the room and then I find the writing comes easily.

After I finish for the night, I walk along the river again to our apartment in SoHo. I will bring home a bottle of Sancerre for Lilly. There is a shop on Little West 12th that stays open late.

"May I pour you another glass?"

"Yes. Have you the escarole this evening?"

"I am sorry. It did not look good to Franco. He purchased several bunches of Swiss chard instead. He is cooking it now. I hope it will be to your liking."

Marchant, some years ago, inherited the café from his brother Bernard, the oldest of three boys. Bernard had suffered a mortal wound in a scuffle with a few young toughs outside a bar on Christopher Street.

He was brought to St. Vincent's. He told the nurse there who cared for him that if he did not survive the surgery, he wanted to leave all his possessions to his younger brother Marchant.

Bernard, a careful and somewhat fearful man, always carried a note to that effect, along with the license to the café and the lease to the family's rent-controlled apartment in a leather wallet sewed into his waistband. He asked the nurse to remove the wallet and begged her to deliver it that night to his brother, which she did at the risk of losing her job or worse.

She was a beautiful woman. Marchant found her quite attractive, and they began seeing one another. A short time later, disgusted with the blood and misery she saw each day in the hospital and finding the young Marchant to be a man of integrity and some kindness, she asked if he would let her work with him in the café.

She had learned to cook at her mother's side in Marseilles, and as Marchant had little facility in the kitchen, he agreed. She soon became indispensable. The business grew. After a while they married, though the marriage did not last long. Long enough, though, for them to have a son they named Franco.

I found myself growing quite hungry. I opened the napkin and placed it across my knees.

Franco makes a very good bouillabaisse.

Marchant got up from his seat. He had some difficulty. He complained of an arthritic hip. His preexisting condition, he called it. Though one evening he shared with me that he had once taken a bad fall in a six-day bike race that unfortunately ended his hopes for the kind of life he had wanted to live.

He returned from the kitchen with the soup, a thick slice of bread, and a small plate of chard.

"Bon appétit," he said.

I told him thank you and he turned back toward the kitchen. He paused, as if thinking of something he had intended to say and either had forgotten or had decided at the end not to.

The breeze off the Hudson had picked up, as it does in the evenings. It came in through the open windows facing the street.

If we don't have rain, I think I might go fishing in the morning and perhaps to the bicycle races in the afternoon.